Embracing BLUE

SHERI ANN SEE

Copyright © 2009 Sheri Ann See
All rights reserved.

ISBN: 1-4392-5684-5
ISBN-13: 9781439256848

See beyond the garden gate

ACKNOWLEDGMENTS

Love and hugs to my husband and children for their great patience and for allowing me the time and space I need and desire to write.

Deep appreciation to my mother for encouraging me to be a writer from the time I was twelve, even though I didn't listen until I was forty and for always believing I would be successful at it.

Purple butterfly kisses and colorful rainbow hugs to my friend Mandy Wells, for proofreading my manuscript.

Most of all sincere gratitude to the universe for allowing me a portion of its spirit to see it, believe it, and bring it to life.

Embracing BLUE

ONE

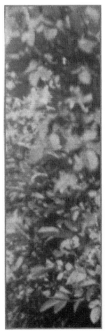

"Hey Len, its Manson, I need a crib where I can disappear, a stretch," the fat ex-con demanded into the telephone.

The worm on the other end of the line was trembling and sweating profusely due to his chronic need for meth.

"I've got somethin' for you, Man, but you're gonna have to travel a piece to get there." Lenny's voice was shaky. "I, I was wonderin' if maybe you could give me a little somethin' in return?" He added carefully, hoping not to piss Manson off.

Manson sneered, knowing his old buddy had it bad. "Yeah, brother, I'll leave you some good stuff under the busted floorboard here in the livin' room. You know the one. Just come by tonight after we're long gone and pick it up, you hear?" He was smug imagining the longtime dope fiend desperately searching for meth, but only finding a meager bag of pot waiting beneath a nest of sleeping copperheads.

The two criminals had lost touch after growing up together in a Missouri military academy until fate reunited them, during Manson's inadequate stint in the state pen for lewd conduct with a minor. He had been working in maintenance at the local grade school and just couldn't keep his hands to himself. Time after time, desperate parents seeking justice had filed charges against him for molesting their children, but only one case was ever brought to trial, thanks to an unexpected eyewitness who happened into the janitor's closet to grab a mop.

The accusations were pouring in again and he was running scared, determined to keep from going back to prison.

"Get the car loaded, woman! We've got to get the hell out of here!" he yelled at his wife, Enid, as he hung up the phone.

"What about Ronny, are we leavin' her behind?" she squeaked, timid as a mouse.

"Hell no, you know she's buildin' that tree house with her girly friend Blue. We're gonna snatch her on the way out of town and put an end to that shit," he snarled.

They tossed the bulk of groceries, linens, and kitchen items into the old sedan before deserting the cockroach-infested rental in Stockton. He drove recklessly, until they were almost to the church then coasted slowly into the parking lot where he stopped the car in the shade to ogle the teenage girls through the dirty windshield. Seeing the two laughing together produced a familiar quiver within him he claimed was his temper flaring, but his wife knew it was his carnal lust for young flesh.

"Look at them makin' their wicked little love nest. God only knows what nasty things they do up there when ain't nobody lookin'," he said to no one in particular, licking his lips at the very thought of it. When his fantasies had run their course, he got out of the car, his weighty footsteps crushing the gravel beneath his boots as he trudged threateningly toward the girls. "Quit embarrassin' us and get your ass in the car!" he rumbled.

His daughter jumped at the sound of his voice, scared to death when she saw him standing below her. "Oh uh, yes, sir, I'm coming!" She wisely obeyed, quickly scrambling down the tree. The moment her feet touched the ground, he grabbed a handful of curls and dragged her across the parking lot before stuffing her into the front seat, confining her between Enid and himself.

Blue jumped from the elevated perch of the oak tree and threw her hammer at the moving car before tumbling to the ground as they sped away in a thick cloud of dust.

* * *

Thunder rolled and lightning clapped like fireworks across the dark Missouri sky as the heavily burdened bucket of bolts transported them down the desolate highway that quickly flooded with the substantial summer downpour.

"We've got to stop and get us a room before I drive us into a ditch. I've been dodgin' turtles all night." Manson swerved off the road when he noticed a *Room for Rent* sign flashing repetitiously at the front entrance of a red brick, two-story house with white shutters flanking each window. "Get in there and rent us that room, woman." He pitched a wad of cash onto his wife's lap.

"But I don't know what to do," Enid complained. "I can't even read. What if they ask me to sign somethin'?"

Manson grabbed a handful of Ronny's thick mane to prevent her from running when Enid opened the door. "Then sign it for hell's sake, and hurry up!" he barked, successfully intimidating her.

She crammed the money into the pockets of her jacket and tried to shield her head from the rain with her small hands. Completely drenched, she stepped apprehensively onto the porch of the neatly kept residence then turned to see her husband anchoring Ronny down with his weight and packing his filthy handkerchief into her mouth to stifle the screams. Enid was more concerned about not knowing how to rent a room than she was about what her husband was doing to their daughter. The brittle creature tapped softly on the door as if she were worried she might wake someone, even though the sports portion of the ten o'clock news blared loudly from the television set inside. When no one came she knocked with more force, knowing Manson would throw a fit if she didn't get the job taken care of quickly.

She shriveled when the porch light glowered down on her and the front door opened, revealing a friendly looking man with white hair and gold wire-framed glasses. Enid noticed his skin was so sheer it was almost purple as he poked his hearing aid into his right ear.

"Can I help you, ma'am?" he asked, noticing her obvious discomfort.

"Oh uh, I was, wantin' to rent your room," she stammered.

"Kind of treacherous weather for a little lady to be out all alone, isn't it?" He squinted, looking out toward the driveway, unable to see beyond the glare and shadows caused by the light reflecting off the rain.

"My husband is out in the car there, you see, and he sent me on account of he isn't feelin' so well," she lied, pulling the crumpled bills from her pockets to keep the man from noticing the two struggling in the front seat.

His curiosity was squelched when he noted her fists were full of cash and he shrugged his shoulders as he took it from her clutches. "Okay do key, just drive on around the back there and you'll find some stairs that'll take you up to the room." He counted the money and added, "This here's just enough for one night, you know. Checkout time is noon tomorrow."

Relieved to be done with it, she scurried down the steps before he could ask any more questions, scooting quickly onto the worn vinyl seat of the car. Manson released Ronny, adjusted his corpulent girth under the steering wheel and fumbled clumsily with the wad of keys in the ignition, leaving her free to escape. She leaped over her mother, fell to the muddy ground and bolted across the swampy backyard, searching frantically for a place to hide.

Manson's anger overtook him as he coasted to the back of the house, barely resisting the urge to run over her. He didn't care that Enid struck her head on the split and sun-faded dashboard when he slammed on the brakes, killing the engine. The veins in his temples pumped fervently as he stumbled to his feet, and his hands curled into fat balls of flesh as he stood, scanning the yard like a ravenous beast, stalking its terrorized prey.

The rain dwindled to a mere drizzle, allowing the moon to illuminate the lawn just enough for him to see a figure slump to the ground near a group of trees along the perimeter of the yard. He drew a deep, satisfying drag from his home-rolled cigarette and a toothless smirk spread across his pudgy face when he exhaled, savoring every thrilling moment of his pursuit. He tossed the butt onto the wet ground, strolling casually behind the car to remove the suitcases from the trunk.

"Well, woman, I guess she's gone for good! We may as well get us some shut-eye and head on out in the mornin'!" he declared loudly enough for the young fugitive to hear him, then leaned in close to his wife and whispered, "Take these bags on up to the room and wait for us."

Enid looked confused, so he held his finger to his lips, instructing her to stay quiet. "Just act natural and do what I told you." He was frustrated with her stupidity and she knew it, so she took the luggage from him and started quickly toward the metal stairway.

Embracing Blue

Manson crouched down on all fours and prowled out into the woods, resembling a wild boar as his underbelly grazed the tips of the tall, slick grass. Enid tried not to stare at her husband who was acting like an animal. Once he was camouflaged by the dark shadows of the trees, he stood to his feet, traveling more swiftly than a man his size should be able to toward his unsuspecting victim.

Ronny could barely make out her mother's slight frame ascending the stairs and decided to stay put until she could be certain both of her parents were inside the room. Intense, sudden pain stabbed sharply at the base of her skull when Manson snuck up behind her and clutched a fistful of curls, forcing Ronny's head back between her shoulders, restricting her ability to scream. His chapped lips brushed against her ear with every indecent proposal he murmured. "Let's just pretend we're one big happy family and maybe I'll go easy on you." Shoving her down onto the soggy ground, he struggled to lay on top of her while she kicked and punched at him, but she could barely move as his oppressive weight became more than she could bear. With one hand, he tugged at his worn leather belt. "One of these days I'm gonna get it through your head that bein' with a real man like me is what God intended." He vowed arrogantly.

Ronny had never grown used to the repugnant obscenities he forced upon her and the last thing she remembered, was the sound of his zipper releasing his fat pod onto her thin, pale torso as the world around her faded graciously to black.

It was barely dawn when the humidity rose from the wet grass. Ronny's vision was blurred from shed tears and endured anguish, as the light of day revealed the aftermath of the night before. Unfamiliar with her surroundings, she tried to focus on the house that was just a short distance away, and flinched when she saw the pedophile lying next to her wearing nothing but a satisfied grin and drool pooling beneath one corner of his mouth. The reality of her life tormented her and grief came swiftly when she realized she was in a strange place without friends to support her. When she tried to sit up, the familiar pain pierced her groin, forcing her backward, landing her head upon her wadded up jeans. Her body convulsed as vomit sprayed from her gut, leaving her vacant, wishing she were dead.

"Don't get, none on you now, darlin', don't want to smell up the car all the way to our new home," her swine of a father mocked, wiping his mouth with the back of his hand.

Ronny wanted nothing more than to get as far away from him as possible and hurried to put on her jeans before pulling on her brown leather boots. Her head swam when she stood, rushing toward him, pounding violently at his back as he struggled to hoist his mass up off the ground.

"When are you going to stop you monster?" She screamed, as he leaned against a tree to support himself as he dressed.

As if she were nothing more than a pesky fly, he ignored her, taking his time with each button of his grass-stained shirt. He noticed the curtains drawing shut in the upstairs window of the house and hoped he could rely on the unspoken don't ask don't tell code some depraved men relied on in such familial matters.

"Now stop screamin'. You're gonna wake those nice folks that rented us the room and they won't never let us come back. We don't want that now, do we, sweetheart?" he patronized her.

"Why? Why do you do this to me?" Ronny tried to scream loud enough to wake her mother.

Manson yawned, bored with her ranting and raving and slowly rolled a cigarette with the papers and tobacco he took from his shirt pocket.

"Now, you know you've always done things different than God intended little girls to do and it's my job as your daddy to bring you up good and proper. We're gonna start by gettin' you out of them boys' clothes you insist on wearin' and into a dress too." He liked putting the blame on her.

"What the hell have I ever done so bad to deserve this?" She was standing up to him for the first time in her life.

Infuriated, he grabbed her by the wrist, squeezing it much too hard. His look of false pity turned into a threatening grimace as he leaned down, almost touching his nose with hers. "You watch your filthy language, little girl. Miss Buhler told us what you and that girly friend of yours have been up to and I promised her I'd get you back on the straight and narrow and that's just what I'm gonna do," he vowed through the venom dripping from his fangs.

"I know why we're running and it's got nothing to do with me! You've been touching little kids again and the police are after your ass is all!" She accused him fearlessly.

Manson decided she wasn't worth the trouble and loosened his grip. "Forget it and get on up to the room before your mother wakes up."

"You're crazy to think I'm going anywhere with you!" She kicked him hard on the shin with the toe of her boot, before sprinting across the lawn, making a beeline for the house. Shocked at her audacity, he tossed his cigarette to the ground and chased after her, limping like a hippo trying to run through mud.

When she finally reached the front porch, she pounded on the door with her fists. "Help, somebody help me, please!"

The door opened and a dim-looking woman wearing a mint green robe and pink sponge rollers in her hair, yawned and stretched, as if nothing unusual was happening.

"What's going on here, missy? Who are you, and what do you want?" She was irritated.

"My mother rented the room from you last night. I need to use your phone. It's my father. I've got to get away from him. Please, just let me use your phone!" Ronny pleaded in desperation, knowing Manson would catch up to her at any moment.

The cotton-topped man from the night before stepped slowly down the stairs inside the house, tying his robe and scratching his head. "Well, I'll be, child. What are you yelling so early in the morning for?"

The exasperating couple provoked Ronny to utter frustration so she closed her eyes and spoke slowly, deliberately, hoping they would take her more seriously. "I have to get away from my father. If I could just use your phone I'll be on my way."

The old man smiled, looking beyond Ronny as he shuffled to the bottom of the stairs and walked right past her, extending his right hand. "Well, good morning to you, mister, I see you're still under the weather. Why, you can't seem to catch your breath."

Ronny gasped as she whirled around to discover Manson standing behind her, clutching his chest and fighting for air.

"Yeah, well, I'll be right as rain soon enough." His labored breathing did nothing to keep him from feigning charm as he effusively pumped the landlord's hand.

"I see you're having a bit of trouble with your youngin here." The ivory-haired man winked at Manson, as if they had a certain understanding between them.

"No! It's not like that. I need your help," she continued to plead.

"Heh heh, you know how teenage daughters like sassin' their daddies. We always get things worked out though, don't we, dumplin'?" His words oozed like sludge from his mouth as he stroked her long, soft spirals with his sinister caress.

The old man chuckled and snuggled up to his wife. "Uh huh, we remember having the same kind of troubles with our own girl when she was this one's age, don't we, Ma?" He reminisced as if it had been a special time in their life together. The decimated woman stared at the braided rug on the floor, unable to reply as memories of her own daughter's cries for help tortured her very soul.

Manson cleared his throat. "Well, sorry we woke you folks. We'll just be on our way and let you two get back to your mornin'."

Gripping Ronny's hand tightly in his, he guided her firmly across the porch, down the steps and to the back of the house. When he heard the door close behind them, he jerked Ronny's arm up between her shoulder blades, making her whimper as they climbed the stairs to the rented apartment where they found Enid snoring contentedly under the covers.

"Wake up, woman, it's time to go! This one is still givin' us troubles." He shoved Ronny forward, yanked the blankets off his slumbering wife and grabbed his rifle from the corner of the room before cocking it and thrusting it at her. "Here, keep this on her while I load the car." He limped down the stairs, still feeling the effects of Ronny kicking him earlier.

Enid aimed the barrel of the gun directly at her daughter, but Ronny assumed she was just playing along until they could both get away. "He's crazy, Mama, this is our chance to get out of here. Pretend you're going to shoot him and let's take the car," she whispered.

Manson returned much more quickly than she thought he would and took the weapon from Enid, then pressed the barrel firmly into the small of Ronny's back, hustling her down the stairs. "You try to run again and I'll shoot your ass."

Ronny believed him and got into the car without a fight. "There's a smart girl." He handed the rifle back to Enid, once she was settled in next to Ronny. "Here, hold onto this. You know what to do if you have to."

He hurried to the driver's seat, turned the key, and pulled discreetly out of the driveway. He was headed for the thick of the Ozarks, where he planned to discipline his daughter the way he wanted to without any hindrance from nosey neighbors.

Ronny refused the sandwich Enid offered her and slept restlessly, as the images of the last two days returned to haunt her. She woke with a start when the car bounced over the roots of the trees that darkened the overgrown forest.

"Where are we?" Enid whined.

Manson slammed on the brakes and proudly spread his arms out wide. "This here's our new home, ladies, Lenny done good, almost makes me wish I'd given him a little more than a bag of weed for such a fine place." He got out of the car to look things over.

Too depressed to care, Ronny sat unmoving, emotionally distraught. Enid craned her head out the window and saw a dilapidated, one-room shack with no foundation and a makeshift porch. A crumbling outhouse sat just behind the old hovel.

"Come on now, get out of the car and start haulin' water from the creek out back and build a fire. I'm gettin' hungry and you girls got to feed me." Manson snickered with wicked satisfaction as he waddled toward the ramshackle water closet, not bothering to close the door before relieving himself with an audible sigh.

His discontented wife moved wearily from the car, faltering before entering the broken-down structure she knew she was expected to transform into a home. One solitary tear rolled down her cheek as she longed for a destiny much different than the cruel one waiting before her.

Ronny took advantage of the fact that her parents had deserted her so thoughtlessly, and grabbed the gun before running away from her demented keepers.

Enid's preoccupation with her dismal future was shattered when she heard the sound of Ronny's footsteps. "Manson? Manson, the girl's runnin'!"

Ronny heard her mother's betrayal and ran faster, hoping the rough and rugged trail would lead her out to the highway soon, but it seemed to be endless.

"Don't worry, old woman. That's the beauty of this place. Ain't nowhere to run and ain't nobody around to hear any screamin' neither!" He announced triumphantly, zipping up his pants.

"But she's got the gun!" Ronny's traitor screeched, afraid to admit she wasn't keeping a closer eye on his hostage.

"I knew you was gonna screw up, dummy, so I took the bullets out of the gun before we even left this mornin'," he scoffed.

Enid was surprised at the unusually good mood he had been in since they pulled into the godforsaken place.

"But what if she gets to the highway and we never see her again?" she worried.

Manson grabbed her roughly by the buttocks, drew her pelvis into his groin, eyeing her suspiciously as he held her close. "You've been mighty helpful in all of this, woman. What's goin' on with you?" He demanded with but a whisper, as he became easily aroused at the mere touch of her paper-thin body.

Repulsed by his unexpected lewdness, Enid stuttered for the right words to say. "Well, you're my husband and

I'm bound by Bible law to do as you tell me to do. I know you're just, wantin' what's best for the girl is all." The harsh truth was, Enid hoped the more he pawed at their adolescent daughter, the less he would want to keep pawing at her. As far as she was concerned, old Buhler had done her a favor and she intended to do whatever it took to make sure Ronny never got away.

"That's right, you are bound by Bible law and I intend to take full advantage of that right now while the girl's away." He almost crushed her when he pinned her between himself and the car, proving his wife's theory to be flimsy at best.

Out in the woods, Ronny stopped running. She was exhausted and needed to gain some sense of direction. She fell wearily to the ground to rest her haggard body against a tick infested tree stump and closed her eyes, trying to imagine what her friends were doing back home. "I know you're worried Blue but I'll get home to you somehow." A tiny flicker of hope sparked within her and she slept until Manson kicked her hard in the hip.

"That's for kickin' me this mornin'!" he sneered. She tottered to her feet, foggy headed but held the rifle squarely on him, squeezing the trigger over and over. "Ha ha, you think I'm stupid, little girl, ain't no ammo in that thing." He opened his hand to reveal several brass bullets and she slowly gave the weapon over to him. He took his sweet time loading the chamber before walking her home and shot a sleeping possum along the way for his wife to dress for supper.

* * *

TWO

Fourteen long years had come and gone, transforming Ronny from a young, sweet girl with a bright future ahead of her, into a grown woman resembling a crazed psychopath, hiding in the shadows of her meager cell.

Her hair was tangled and knotted, her fingernails brittle and yellowed, and her skin that was once the color of sugar cookies, was stained black from too many years of hard labor and nowhere but the grimy creek to take a bath.

It was difficult for her to believe how long it had been since that first futile attempt to escape. So many times she had tried to flee since then, only to have Enid catch her and turn her in to

Manson, the guard of the desolate prison. One time, Enid caught her sneaking out in the middle of the night and screeched as if the house were on fire, until Manson woke up and taught Ronny a lesson in his most favorite way.

Another time, when Manson was out back working on the still, Ronny swiped the car keys from the pocket of his jacket that hung by the door, but he heard the engine and came running with Enid nipping obediently at his heels. Ronny had long ago surrendered all hope of Enid ever rushing in to rescue her when she realized the click, click, clicking sound coming from the other side of the sheet that divided the room, was that of her mothers' knitting needles.

I could have done more to stop him, tried harder to escape, she mistakenly told herself.

How many times had Manson come skulking to her corner of the room, mauling and raping her in his professed attempt to transform her into what he considered to be normal, she could not fathom. How many ill-begotten babies had been mercifully miscarried from her body long before they ever developed fully in the womb, she did not know.

She shivered in the darkness, sweat drenching her clothes as she gripped the butcher knife her mother had used to end her own life, only days before. The image of Enid's wisp of a body lying rigid on the floor, blood draining from her wrists, was still vivid in Ronny's mind.

The sound of Manson blundering through the front door startled her back to the present. "Come to Daddy, sweetheart! Your mama's gone; now we don't have to hide no more!" He slurred, dumping the day's kill onto the counter. "Why the hell's it so dark in here? Light a lamp, damn it!" He opened the empty icebox, expecting to see a plate full of left over possum and sweet potatoes, but there was none, for Ronny had decided the last thing she would ever serve her bastard of a father, was justice. "How's come you ain't out here servin' me my dinner, you damned ungrateful..." He chugged more moonshine from the gallon jug. It was obvious he had already had too much to drink and would come for her just as he had always done since she was, God only knew how young. She stiffened and her throat burned from the bile that rose from her gut, when she saw his shadow on the other side of the sheet coming toward her. Manson moved past her, tucking his thumbs under his suspenders and pulled them from his broad shoulders before dropping solidly to his knees beside her stained and tattered mattress. "Why you ain't waitin' up for me? Huh? Little girl of mine?" he taunted her as he unzipped his pants before removing the pungent, sweat stained T-shirt over his head and tossing it to the floor. She watched him, disgusted at the sight of his grotesquely obese body that was covered in a blanket of coarse gray fur. "Now that's more like it." He drawled lasciviously as he groped the pillow, searching for her breast in his drunken stupor. "What the hell?" He swore vehemently when he realized the bed was empty.

"You will never touch me again, old man!" Ronny screamed, as she charged toward his back with the blade poised high above her head, aiming to strike him between the shoulders.

Manson turned, his arms raised instinctively, thwarting her attempt to kill him as the knife propelled through the air, landing with a thud on the floor.

"What the hell you think you're doin', little girl? You belong to me now that your mother's gone, and it's your duty to take care of me. That's just the way things are and how they're gonna stay." He claimed, as if it were a matter of fact.

"It's my *duty*? And just what was your excuse *before* she took her own life? No! This is *not* how things are going to stay. Not for me. You have taken as much from me as you are going to get!" She screamed as her hand landed with a firm slap across his face.

Manson rubbed his beet-red cheek, amused by his feisty daughter's gamble and he laughed out loud at her boldness.

Ronny searched frantically for the knife and Manson tripped her to the solid mud floor, knocking the wind out of her when she landed severely on her belly.

He positioned himself behind her and clutched her slight waist in his powerful hands, causing her to scream.

"Ain't nobody ever heard you hollerin' all the way out here and you know it." Manson relished such moments and he laid his weight prostrate on her back, wheezing the dank vapor of his breath on her skin. The cool of the dirt floor on her cheek was commonplace as he skillfully manipulated the skirt of her dress up around her hips, coercing her buttocks effortlessly into his crotch. Breathless with excitement, he moaned deep and low when he nestled his face brusquely into her thick tresses at the back of her neck. Ronny could barely breathe, and her body jerked as she gagged from the stench of possum grease and whiskey exuding from his pores, and he mistook her disgust for pleasure. "Why you still fight me, darlin'?" His voice was full of gravel and he panted like a dog as he dominated her over and over again before passing out, face down, with half his body anchoring her to the floor.

Impotent and deflated, she strained to get out from under him and rolled onto her side to heave. It felt good to be able to breathe after a long night of being smothered by his weight. His loud snoring meant he was in a deep sleep but she knew she had to act fast. Groggily, she stood to her feet, giving the blood time to find her brain, and noticed the weapon lying on the floor. Reaching down carefully, she held her breath, trying not to wake him. She surprised herself when she grabbed the knife, straddled his back, and plunged the steel blade deep into his thick hide, once and then again, leaving it there while he squealed like a stuck pig. Time stood still, as she leaned forward and whispered in his ear, her voice hoarse, her words concise, "I told you, *never* again, old man."

The squealing stopped, and Manson went limp. Ronny felt numb from the neck down unable to believe she was truly free from the shackles put on her by the demon lying motionless beneath her.

Too weak to stand, she crawled to the front door then stumbled out to the creek, ripping the bloody, threadbare dress from her body as she fell into the shallow, muddy water. She lay there a long time, dazed, watching her father's vital fluids rush downstream before returning to the ghostly shack.

As she stepped warily over the bloody corpse, she became aware of her own blood coursing through her veins.

A pillow case waited in the corner behind her mattress and she opened it to find her faded blue jeans inside, just as she had left them so long ago. The musty smell of denim reminded her of the girl she used to be and when she put them on they hung loose on her gaunt, overused form. Her hands were shaking as she buttoned her dingy shirt and the once soft, brown leather boots were stiff from lack of use as she slid one onto each foot. The familiar clothes felt good against her skin and she began to feel like nothing stood between her and Blue, except the miles.

Ronny eased toward Manson to take the car keys from the pocket of his pants that were still entangled around his ankles and she imagined he was going to come back to life and grab her as she reached in, but she was relieved when her finger hooked the ring and she pulled them out.

Without stopping to think whether she should or shouldn't, she ripped the old sheet down that divided the shack in half and threw it on top of Manson's lifeless body. Next, she grabbed the jug of hooch off the counter and dumped some onto the mattress that had for so long served as his crime scene then emptied the rest onto Manson, before striking a match from the book she found in his shirt pocket. When she tossed it onto the sheet, the flames jumped up at her, and she moved unhurried to the car. She turned the key in the ignition, but the engine only chugged and gurgled as she pumped the accelerator. Smoke rolled out the door, but she remained calm, and punched the gas pedal with too much force, killing the engine. As the reality of what she had done hit her between the eyes, her body shook uncontrollably and she tried to start the car again, this time

Embracing Blue

pressing down on the pedal gently. The console lights glowed dim, but promising, and she slid the gearshift into **D** like she had seen Manson do and the car moved forward, sputtering down the rough and rugged lane.

As she passed the modest mound of dirt that covered Enid's body, Ronny wished she'd had the sort of mother daughters wept for when they died.

Black smoke coming from the exhaust pipe followed her as she continued down the trail of dirt and weeds, not knowing where it would lead. It must have been at least ten miles before she reached the highway. *No wonder I never got anywhere when I ran.*

The old sedan threatened to quit on her again. "Please. *Please* don't die on me here!" She yelled, coasting to a complete stop. Cranking the key and pumping the gas pedal only flooded the engine. "OOH! You piece of junk!" She hit the dash with the palm of her hand and cried with her head on the steering wheel. "Which way do I go, Blue? Which way will lead me home?" She turned the key one more time. The engine choked but she ignored it, suddenly absolutely certain which way she should go, but the metal carcass only carried her about a mile down the highway before it hissed its last breath. Ronny finally gave up trying to save it and left it on the side of the road, painfully aware of the sweltering heat as she wandered aimlessly down the long stretch of blacktop. Perspiration poured from her head and the humidity was stifling, drenching her aching body. Ronny felt sick to her stomach and stumbled as the landscape blurred before her.

* * *

THREE

At the edge of beautiful Stockton Lake Eva Johnson joined her daddy, Sanford, on the front porch of their spacious log home, and handed him a cup of black coffee before sitting opposite him on the whitewashed swing with the olive green and white striped cushions.

"Well now, Eva girl. What are you doing out here with me, instead of helping your mama and Sissy in the kitchen?" he teased.

"Considering what day this is, they just won't hear of me lifting a finger to help them." Eva took a drawing pad and stick of charcoal from the canvas pouch that hung off the arm of the swing.

Sanford rubbed his chin. "Just what's so special about today anyhow? I've never heard of your mother refusing help from *anybody* in the kitchen."

"Now, Daddy, you know it's my birthday. Don't play like you don't," Eva reproved him.

"Oh yeah, that's right. Well I knew it had to be something very important for you to be getting out of doing your chores." he puffed contentedly on his pipe and his sapphire eyes crinkled around the edges when he grinned. "Yeah, girl of mine, it's good to be home and not have to work at the mill today, of all days."

Eva inhaled the sweet scent of Virginia tobacco that always brought to mind her mama's homemade maple syrup. "I'm glad you're home this year too, Daddy, it's been a few."

"Well, get used to having me underfoot more than usual. Mr. Farnsworth hired a young man that's strong as an ox and as long as he's around, I won't need to work anymore than what's fair and necessary."

The comforting sound of Eva's mama Belle and sister Sissy working in the kitchen was interrupted when the telephone rang.

"Wonder who that is calling?" Eva tried to eavesdrop.

"I'll bet it's our Billy and Zoey, you know they call every year to wish you a happy birthday." Sanford guessed.

"Probably so, I need to make a trip out to their place sometime soon," she said thoughtfully as she sketched.

"I know they sure do love it when you take time to visit. They mean a lot to your mother and me, darling. I want you to always remember that. If something were to ever happen to us, you'd know who to turn to, wouldn't you?" Sanford was serious.

"Yeah Daddy, I would." Eva returned her things to the bag before wiping her blackened fingertips on the cloth inside.

Sanford was hungry and the delicious smells coming from the kitchen were distracting to him. "Ooh, Eva girl, my mouth is starting to water. I hope we don't have to wait much longer."

"Me neither. I can already taste the blackberry jam." Eva's tummy growled.

"Speaking of blackberries, the bushes should be full about now. We're going to have to get to picking before they go to the chiggers or get burnt up by the sun," he reminded her.

Eva frowned. "Ooh! My fingers grow numb just thinking about those darn berries. I hate the sweat running down my neck and the dirt sticking to the backs of my knees."

Sanford clenched his pipe between his teeth, trying not to chuckle at his daughter's flair for the dramatic. "Yes, darling, you do suffer so every year, I know," he sympathized sarcastically.

Eva was so used to him being ornery she stubbornly ignored him and continued. "Of course when Mama bakes up a cobbler or puts the first jar of preserves on the table, it suddenly seems worth all the trouble. Guess it's just one of those things a *child* swears she hates and grows to be a young *woman* recalling it to mind as a time she holds near and dear." she smacked a mosquito on her arm then wiped its guts directly on the skirt of her white and yellow checked sundress.

Sanford looked mischievously at his daughter. "Just who is this *woman* you're talking about?"

"Well, me of course, Daddy! After all, it is my fourteenth birthday and I suppose it's time I start acting my age. You know, more mature like, don't you expect?" Eva charmed him, straightening her posture and smoothing her hair, hoping to look more sophisticated than she really felt.

"Well now, maybe you are growing up, Eva girl. Sure you're not going on twenty today?" Sanford couldn't help but notice how much she looked like him, and the resemblance between them grew stronger with each passing birthday. They had the same chin, nose even their long, slender fingers were identical. But her petite figure, green eyes, light brown skin, and full lips with the natural pout, she inherited from someone else entirely.

His thoughts were shattered by the shrill screech of the screen door. "Come and get it!" Sissy bellowed.

Eva covered her ears with both hands. "Now, Sissy child, we're right here. There is no good reason for you to be hollering so." They both stuck their tongues out at one another and giggled, as they walked arm in arm behind Sanford, letting the screen door slam behind them.

The sight of the picture-perfect table took Eva's breath away. It was draped in a bleached white oilcloth adorned with the green and pink Depression glass her mama almost never used. Large, ceramic serving platters were heaped with baking soda biscuits, country sausage, black pepper bacon, wheat cakes, and eggs fried sunny-side up. Tumblers filled to the brim with gravy, raw honey, real sugar cane molasses, and maple syrup tapped from the trees outside bridged the gaps between the platters of food. It was all a nice change from the usual boiled grits.

There was no room on the table for the lemon birthday cake; with the white coconut frosting that drifted like snow so it sat alone on the kitchen counter.

"Oh, Mama, you've gone and made my favorite again this year." Eva reached toward the tempting desert for a finger full of the fluffy white cream.

Belle gave her a look that warned her to step away from temptation, and she did so immediately.

"Girl, you know we won't be cutting into it until later when your grandparents get here. I only set it out to show you what a fine job your sister did helping me make it." Belle explained, hugging her daughter close.

Eva smiled warmly at Sissy. "Thank you, little sister of mine. The cake is simply a work of art, and so is this table. You must be growing up or something, huh?" Sissy blushed at the compliment from her older sister she admired so much.

Sanford was in the living room emptying his pipe into an already full ashtray that was smooth in some places, and bumpy in others. He was remembering when Eva had brought it home from school years ago, a gift she had made him for Father's Day.

"Sanford, come on now, this food's about to get cold. Have a seat here next to the birthday girl and give thanks for this fine meal, won't you?" Belle spoke in her calm, unruffled way before taking her seat at the end of the table.

Sanford understood how important this ritual was to his wife and folded his hands respectfully in front of him. "I would be honored to do so, my Belle."

Eva sat across the table from her sister and Belle saw the girls roll their eyes at one another before reverently bowing their heads.

The moment Sanford finished with the expected amen, Sissy grabbed a biscuit before passing the platter to her mother. Eva leaped from her seat to get the metal pitcher that always held the fresh, cold milk and filled each person's glass before setting it on the table to continue grappling and passing the grub.

"Now, what was that look you two were giving one another when your daddy started praying?" Belle tried to be annoyed with her daughters' irreverence.

The young girls looked wide-eyed at one another, silently reproving themselves for getting caught. "Huh? I don't know what you mean, Mama." Eva picked up her fork, scanning the table to see what she may have missed.

"Me neither." Sissy pierced a slimy egg with her biscuit, scooped up the runny, yellow yoke, and sloshed it to her lips, dripping some on her chin then gulped it all down with a swig of milk before wiping her mouth with the skirt of her dress. Clearly irritated, Belle held out a white linen napkin to her youngest that had been lying unnoticed beside the child's plate all along.

"Thank you, Mama." Sissy smacked her lips and used the cloth to smear the grease from her mouth, out onto her cheeks, before crumpling it in her fist. When she tossed it onto the table, one corner was left to dangle in the gravy boat and Belle scowled at her, wishing she would pay more attention.

Eva snickered at her entertaining sister. "I was just thinking that instead of praying with words, we could be thanking God for this fine meal by making a full-blown mess of ourselves like Sissy's doing right now. There's no doubt she appreciates it."

The girls laughed, which made Belle more exasperated with Sissy who was still tackling the food on her plate. "And what about you, do you agree with your sister here?"

Sissy licked each finger before answering her mother. "Yes, ma'am, I surely do. I mean, doesn't God know we like the food?"

"Yes, I suppose so, but we should always say thank you and be grateful." Belle reasoned with them.

Eva felt her mother was making too much of it, and for as long as she had been old enough to consider such matters, she'd suspected her mother had gotten very good at pretending to be someone she really wasn't.

Sanford cleared his throat before speaking up. "Now, I'm sure the girls mean no disrespect, Belle. They just have their own way of looking at things, is, all. Everybody has their own way of praying. That's all right isn't it?"

Belle relaxed a bit, and tipped the platter in front of her to slide a greasy fried egg onto her plate. "All right then, we'll save this for another time being it's Eva's birthday and all but we *will* discuss it," she promised weakly, only halfway meaning what she said.

Sissy squealed, making Belle jump. "Ooh, this is just *begging* for some blackberry jam!" she spooned some onto her second yoke stained biscuit, completely unaware she had startled her mother so. Belle closed her eyes, massaging her temples like all mothers do when they have reached the final limit with their children.

"Girl of mine, I swear," Sanford warned his youngest. Sissy just happened to notice Eva and Sanford scowling at her as she stretched across the table, aiming for the molasses.

"What?" She blinked her Kewpie doll eyes, oblivious to the show she had just put on for her family.

Fatigued, Belle rubbed her brow, speaking sedately, not wanting to aggravate her pounding headache. "It's all right. I've just been under a load lately is, all. Go on and eat now. I'm fine."

Wanting to change the subject, Sanford raised his transparent rose-colored milk glass. "Well, ladies, why don't we sing happy birthday to our Eva girl before she grows to be another year older?"

The three of them sang the old familiar tune, although Belle sang with less enthusiasm, thinking of younger days long before babies and birthday parties.

"Thank you, thank you," Sissy gushed, bowing dramatically.

Sanford ate until he was full, and rubbed his swollen belly. "My Belle, you have done it again. Mm-*MM* I do believe this was the very best birthday meal you have ever made."

Belle didn't reply, she was preoccupied with her daydreams and she turned her attention to Eva without really seeing her. "Oh, that was Miss Billy on the telephone earlier. Says she hopes you can stop by in the next day or two and pick up the special gift they have for you."

A car pulled into the drive, stirring up the dust and Belle felt overwhelmed at the idea of Sanford's parents coming over. "Oh! It's Grammy Blanche and Grand

Daddy Roy," Sissy cheeped, and the girls rushed out the door to greet them.

Sanford's parents stepped from the freshly waxed, black with silver trim, Cadillac. Roy pulled the many cellophane-wrapped birthday gifts from the back seat, and Blanche slammed her door shut with more force than was necessary before stretching her short flabby arms out wide, inviting the girls to collect their hugs. "Come to Grammy, children!"

Miss Blanche was a plenteous woman, with caramel brown skin and flaming, red from a box, hair. Her brilliant blue eyes hid behind her chubby cheeks when she smiled, and the rings on her pudgy fingers were garnished with every stone a girl could imagine, and some she never could. Her breasts were huge, and her collar was low, so when the small girls accepted their Grandma's, loving embrace they were swallowed up in the abyss of her bountiful bosom.

"Well, happy birthday, Darling!" she drawled in her sufficiently rehearsed baby talk then planted a kiss on Eva's cheek, leaving perfect lip prints in the shade of Siren Red.

Eva gasped for air, "Thank you, Grammy Blanche."

"Hey there, Grand daddy Roy," the girls hollered in unison, extracting themselves from Blanche's viselike grip. Roy wiggled his fingers hello from behind the awkward load he was still trying to balance in his arms.

"Howdy, darlings," he replied.

Roy was a long, thin, extremely patient man. His tan slacks were pressed with a severe crease down the front and back, breaking precisely at the top of his newly polished boots. His coal-black skin showed off his plain gold wedding band and his nails were impeccably manicured. Blanche insisted he look his best at all times, even though he felt silly sitting next to her at the salon having his nails buffed to a high sheen.

Eva and Sissy rushed to the other side of the car, taking several packages from Roy. "Let us help you with these things. You two come in out of the heat now," Eva offered considerately.

Blanche reached inside the window, plucked her purse from the front seat, and strolled toward the house like a big, but not too tall, fashion model working the catwalk. Sissy and Eva tried to suppress a giggle, knowing they would be secretly whispering about their Grandmother at bedtime.

"Well *where,* is your mama and daddy? Sanford, Belle?" Blanche squawked, disappointed her very own son and daughter in law had failed to come outside with the girls to meet them.

Belle opened the screen door, as they paraded into the house with Roy towing the end of the line. "Hello, Roy, Blanche," she greeted them, forcing a smile.

"Hey there, Miss Belle," Roy stopped to kiss her on the cheek.

"Let me help you with those, Pop," Sanford offered, taking the packages from his father. Roy steadied himself on the arm of the sofa before sitting down.

"Well, son of mine, come and give your mama a big hug, sweetheart," Blanche effused, in her usual high shrill.

Sanford moved toward his mother, stretching his arms as far around her curvaceous figure as they would go and gave her a quick peck on the cheek. "Hey now, Mama, you're looking lovely as ever."

Blanche reeled at the compliment from her only son she adored more than life itself. "Belle, how are you doing? You're looking a might pale this morning, sugar, everything all right," Blanche pried, inspecting her from head to toe.

Belle ignored the question and welcomed their guests hospitably. "Can I offer you a chair, Blanche?"

As if she had done a hard day's work, Blanche sat down heavily. "Oh yes, yes, please girl. Well, it looks like we're just in time for breakfast. Ooh, are those wheat cakes I see all the way down there at the *other* end of the table?" Blanche rooted her nose in the air, like a pig searching for slop.

Belle held her composure, even though she had no idea they intended on joining them for breakfast as well as birthday cake. "Where are my manners? Can I fix you two a plate? We started a bit early is, all."

Roy patted his small paunch of a belly. "Oh no, we had an early breakfast at Moe's diner this morning, Belle."

Blanche threw him a glowering look, then quickly turned back to face her hostess, smiling more broadly than was natural for anyone who wasn't a Cheshire.

"Well, maybe just a little something. I had a light snack is all and the long drive over here has left me nearly famished, if you don't mind, that is." she held her sausage-like fingers daintily at her jeweled throat, letting her words drip sweeter than honey.

Belle grinned wryly at Roy and pulled a clean plate and two glasses from the cupboard. "Sweet tea, Roy?" she offered.

"Well now, that is one thing I never turn down this time of year. Yes, thank you much," Roy accepted graciously.

"Why don't we, go on out to the porch, Pop?" Sanford suggested now glad for the company.

"Sounds like a good idea, son." Roy rocked back and forth, trying to build momentum under his lightweight body and stood, taking a moment to gain his balance before following Sanford outside.

Sanford kissed Belle lightly. "Thank you again for the fine meal."

Belle pressed two fingers to the warm spot on her lips. "Uh, you're welcome, Sanford. I'll be out with your tea in just a shake."

Blanche eyed her suspiciously, as she poked two slices of cold bacon into her mouth.

Out on the porch, Sanford sat in his favorite chair and his father sat in the swing. "Whoo-ee, the humidity's getting thick for sure, eh son?" Roy wiped his brow with a freshly ironed black and white paisley handkerchief he took from his shirt pocket.

Eva rushed out to the porch; arms piled high with her new things, letting the screen door slam behind her. "Ooh, Daddy. Just look at these beautiful dresses and hair bows Grandma and Grand daddy brought me!" she exclaimed.

Roy clutched his chest, slumping backward in the swing. "Eva girl, one of these days you're going to give this old man a heart attack slamming that door the way you do."

"Oh. Sorry Grand daddy. It's a habit with all of us around here," she apologized.

"So I have noticed, little lady, so I have noticed," Roy teased, happy she was so pleased with her gifts. He blushed when Eva bent down and kissed him on the cheek.

"I have never seen such beautiful clothes in all my life." she gushed with delight.

Roy recovered quickly from his heart attack and smiled fondly at his oldest granddaughter. "Well you've never been fourteen years old before, young lady."

"I can't wait to try this one on. Can I, Daddy?" she held the yellow dress up, unable to stand still.

"I think that's a great idea, birthday girl. You come on out here and show us how it all comes together, you hear?" he told her as she kissed him before running back into the house.

"Sorry, Grand daddy!" she hollered over her shoulder as the screen door slammed again behind her.

The two men chuckled. "She always could bring a smile to your face, couldn't she, boy?" Roy struck a match on his boot and lit his pipe.

"Yes sir-ee, Pop, she always could," Sanford said, lighting his own.

Eva returned wearing the most beautiful yellow chiffon dress, with a small matching bow clipped to her hair. Sanford sat up straight and gaped at the lovely vision of someone he knew long ago.

Puzzled by her father's expression, she closed the screen gently behind her. "Are you all right, Daddy?"

Sanford's mouth went dry, and he swallowed hard. "Yes, yes, darling I'm just fine."

Belle joined them on the porch and set a tray of refreshments on the small table before taking a seat next to him.

"Well, Mama?" Eva waited for her mother's approval.

Belle stared at the young girl draped in sunshine and knew exactly what Sanford was thinking.

"Mama, what's wrong?" Eva started to feel self-conscious.

"Huh? Oh, you look beautiful, Eva, just like a dream." Belle poured the tea, handing everyone a glass, hoping she hadn't been too obvious.

Sissy came out to the porch, not realizing Blanche was right behind her, and let go of the screen. When she saw Roy brace himself, for the expected racket, she turned quickly to grab it, but Blanche stopped it just in time with the pointed toe of her too tight, leather shoe. "Thank you, Grammy," she sighed with relief.

"Why, you're welcome, sugar," Blanche replied good- naturedly. Roy wiped the sweat from his brow, and stretched his arm around Sissy when she took a seat next to him. Blanche smiled, kicked the door wide open then waddled out onto the porch without the slightest attempt to slow it down and, *BAM!* Roy grabbed his chest, scowling at his wife who responded with only a pat on the leg, directing him to scoot over. He was incredulous as she forced her wide derriere between him and the arm of the swing, landing solidly with a grunt.

"Why are you and Mama looking at me so funny like, Daddy?" Eva sat on the arm of Sanford's chair.

Belle handed a glass of tea to Blanche and Sissy and wondered how her husband was going to answer their daughter's question.

"You're growing up so fast, sweetheart, we just aren't ready for it," he was only half honest.

Blanche yanked her white lace hanky out of her plunging cleavage, and held it at the end of her pug nose as if she had been anxiously awaiting a dramatic opportunity such as this to use the affect. "You two are just so cute together I just can't stand it!" she whimpered theatrically.

Everyone looked at her as if she had lost her mind and Belle never had the patience for one of Blanche's performances. "Birthday cake and ice cream anyone?" she pretended the moment hadn't turned awkward and uncomfortable.

Blanche's eyes brightened and she promptly tucked her hanky back into her brassiere, struggling to stand from the swing. She couldn't quite get to her feet and fell back into the cushion, making a childish pouty face at Roy who was also trying to stand while she bounced and jostled around. "Sit still now, Blanche. I'll grab you in a minute," he chided her.

When she settled down, the swing did too, making it possible for him to stand and face her. He took her glass and set it on the tray then grasped both of her hands, straining as he leaned backward. His face turned red and the sweat streamed down his face, so Sanford stepped in to help his father and together they pulled her up and out.

Roy wheezed and grabbed the chain of the swing, trying to catch his breath after towing the wide load, while Blanche hurried past him. "Come on, Roy! What are you waiting for? There's no need to be rude now, let's get on into the house and have some of that cake Belle's offering."

Roy sighed and followed his wife inside. He took the door from her as if she were a child losing a privilege and closed it gently behind them. Blanche furrowed her brow, disappointed she wasn't allowed to let the door slam and, like a spoiled toddler, she huffed and jutted her chin into the air, stomping all the way into the dining room.

Belle and the girls were already inside clearing the breakfast dishes and preparing the table for the dessert. "Sissy, you bring the cake, please, and Eva, you get the ice cream from the freezer," Belle instructed them.

Blanche grabbed a handful of forks and spoons out of the silverware drawer and laid them in a heap. Belle brought the small saucers and server, while Sissy set the cake in the center of the table.

"Well, sugar, you want us to sing you a song again, now that your grandma and grand daddy are here?" Sanford asked Eva.

"No, Daddy, I say we just dig in," Eva replied, eager to taste the cake.

"Oh goodie," Blanche said as she reached across the table to grab the cake server and thrust it at Belle. "Sissy girl, you pass the forks now, and I expect your mother will be doing the cutting. Right, Belle?" Blanche fluttered her false eyelashes and smiled, as if she had the whole canary between her cheeks. Belle tried to be humored by her mother-in-law's ways, but some days were just more difficult to be so than others. Afraid she might lose her temper if she replied, she cut into the cake without a word, worried Blanche might perish if she didn't eat soon.

When everyone had been served, Belle's thoughts wandered again to a time in her life when she was young and in love, but not with her husband. *Sanford could tell their marriage was coming to an end, couldn't he? It was so obvious...wasn't it?*

"What's going on with you, Belle? You just haven't been yourself since we got here," Blanche continued to meddle, dumping a spoonful of ice cream into her mouth.

Belle longed for some time alone. "I'll make us some coffee," her voice quivered.

Blanche watched her with raised eyebrows, spoon protruding from the pucker of her lips as Belle rushed past the percolator and down the hallway, tears filling her lower lids.

"Blue Belle," Sanford stood and reached out to her but she ran into the bathroom, locking the door behind her. She turned on the bathtub faucet but it did little to drown the sounds of her sorrow, as she sat on the cool linoleum floor and pulled a silver heart shaped locket from the high collar of her dress. This was as close as she ever got to being with her true love anymore. A rare moment or two, stolen each day to gaze at the tiny photograph of the curly headed girl with the soft white skin and the radiant smile she had lost so very long ago.

* * *

FOUR

Ronny's sight grew dim and her body ached as it never had before. The sickening smell of her kerosene-saturated skin was strong, from the many years of fighting off the ticks and chiggers. The sweat continued to stream from her pores and she collapsed in the blazing Missouri heat.

"Harold! Somebody's lying on the side of the road!" the woman in the approaching RV hollered to her husband. He slowed and pulled over and she jumped from the vehicle, rushing to Ronny's side to check her pulse. "She's alive! Bring some cold water and washcloths, she's burning up!" The man poured water from a gallon jug into a bucket and met his wife who was kneeling beside Ronny. He dipped a cloth into the water then laid it on her forehead and his wife lifted her shirt to wet her belly. "Uh oh, Harold, look at this," she said anxiously.

"Oh boy, it's a bull's-eye. This poor girl has Lyme disease, Hazel." Harold lifted Ronny's head and squeezed water into her mouth and she coughed a little, barely regaining consciousness.

The woman pulled Ronny's shirt down to cover the rash. "Are you all right, honey?" Ronny was delirious and disoriented, babbling gibberish as far as the older couple could tell. "She needs a doctor, Harold. She's obviously been in this heat far too long."

Harold didn't hesitate before putting Ronny over one shoulder and carrying her to the RV. "Skinny little thing. I bet she doesn't weigh an ounce."

"There's no doubt she's been through something terrible. I bet her head is just full of ticks hiding in all that knotted hair, although I can't imagine they would want to go anywhere near her. She smells like she's been bathing in kerosene." Hazel opened the door for her husband and he laid Ronny on a plush leather seat in the back of the rig.

The kind woman stayed by Ronny's side and continued to wash her down with cool water, while Harold drove to the nearest hospital. Ronny prattled on as if she were replaying the last fourteen years in her mind making the older couple wonder what in God's name the haggard young woman had been through.

"I wish she could tell us how she got those bruises all over her body," Harold said sadly.

"It's obvious she's severely dehydrated and hasn't eaten much in a very long while too," Hazel replied.

When they pulled into the emergency entrance, Harold carried Ronny inside while Hazel explained the situation to the nurse at the front desk. Two aides came right away and put Ronny onto a gurney before carting her off behind the swinging doors.

Harold put his arm around his tenderhearted wife's shoulders and helped her to a chair. "She'll be just fine, dear. She's in good hands now." They took a seat in the waiting room and both fell asleep, Hazel with her head on Harold's chest.

"Mr. and Mrs. Montgomery," the doctor woke the sleeping couple. "I'm Dr. Callahan."

"Oh, yes, Doctor. How is the girl?" Harold asked, standing to his feet. Hazel stayed seated, hoping for good news.

"I wouldn't normally be able to give you any information about the patient since you aren't related to her, but since you're the ones who found her and she has no identification I'll make an exception. First, I need to know if you will be taking responsibility for her," he said.

"What do you mean by responsibility?" Harold wasn't sure just what he was asking of them.

"Yes, of course we will," Hazel spoke up without a second thought, barely glancing at her husband. "Is she going to be all right?"

Harold sighed and closed his eyes, knowing her mind was made up. The doctor waited for confirmation that he was in agreement with his wife's decision and Harold nodded his head warily.

"Good. We have her on intravenous antibiotics and she will need to be so, for at least two days. You were right about the Lyme disease, but hopefully we caught it soon enough that she won't suffer any lasting effects from it. Time will tell, but we will be sending her home with a prescription she'll need to take for a month or longer. I'll give you a tube of hydrocortisone cream as well, for those nasty chigger bites." He grew somber and sat down beside Hazel, motioning Harold to take a seat as well. He spoke quietly, confidentially. "She's going to need a lot of care when she leaves here. We discovered a lot of bruising."

"Yes, we noticed that too," Hazel spoke up wishing her hunch of abuse would have been a mistake.

Dr. Callahan continued hesitantly. "I mean on the inside, as well as the outside."

Hazel gulped, and Harold hung his head. "What are you saying, Doctor?" Hazel was afraid she already knew the answer.

"Look, we have her on an IV to hydrate her, and as soon as she's able, she'll need to start eating a healthy diet. She's practically starved herself, but she will also be needing help for the troubles we can't see. Someone has been raping her for many years." He said bluntly. "Did she say anything when you were with her that might help us know who has done this to her?"

"She was sort of rambling about something, but not really making any sense. We thought it was the fever talking." Harold regretted he hadn't paid better attention to what she had said.

"Something she said made me think her parents are both dead. Yes, something about a fire. Oh, I can't be sure." Hazel tried to help.

Dr. Callahan spoke with great control over his anger. "Well, someone needs to pay for the crimes committed on this unfortunate soul. Maybe once she recovers she'll be able to tell you something. If she does, you need to report it to the police as soon as possible. Meanwhile, I'm going to write a report myself and turn it into the authorities."

"When can we take her home?" Hazel asked anxiously.

"In a couple of days if I can see she's responding well to the antibiotics, if not, maybe a couple of weeks. You folks are good to take her in. I'll talk to you soon." Dr. Callahan shook both of their hands and turned to leave.

Hazel looked Harold in the eye for the first time since offering to take care of Ronny, and he hugged her close.

"I don't know what you've gotten us into this time, but you did the right thing by speaking up for the girl. Come on. Let's go home and get cleaned up. I know you'll want to get back here as soon as possible." He knew his wife well.

Hazel kissed him on the cheek, reminded of why she loved him so much.

* * *

FIVE

*I*t was a full week before Ronny was released from the hospital. She was depressed and thinner than ever, but her fever had broken and she was able to speak more rationally, although she barely spoke at all.

"Well, good morning, young lady," Hazel greeted her softly.

Ronny sat in a wheelchair staring out the window and didn't have the strength to turn around to see who was speaking to her.

Harold stayed by the bed as Hazel approached Ronny slowly from behind and sat on the windowsill to face her. "My name is Hazel. My husband, Harold, and I are the ones who brought you here last week." Ronny wasn't sure just how to respond to the kind strangers who had saved her life. Hazel sensed her discomfort and wanted nothing more than to put her at ease. "You don't know us, but we've become mighty attached to you." She continued to try.

Harold wondered if maybe this was a bad idea and sat beside his wife to see what he could do to help. "Do you have any family, honey? Is there someone else we should call to come and get you?" Ronny looked at Harold, barely shaking her head no. "Will you permit us to take you home and care for you?" Harold asked gently.

Ronny nodded her head and her eyes seemed to smile at him, although her expression never changed.

Hazel was relieved when Ronny responded to her husband. "OK, then, let's go home," Hazel beamed as she took the handles of the chair, wheeling Ronny to the door then giving it up to a nurse who wheeled her to the elevator.

They brought the RV so Ronny would have plenty of room to lie down in the back if she needed to, but she was able to sit upright, directly behind Hazel. Harold helped her get comfortable before assisting Hazel up into the front seat and Ronny thought she had died and gone to heaven when the cool breeze from the air conditioner kissed her skin. They rode home in silence and she watched the trees flash by, lulling her into a much needed sleep.

When they pulled into the circle drive, Harold and Hazel tried not to wake their guest when they got out of the RV. "She needs us, Harold, I can feel it. Fate brought us together and I'm not turning my back on her. Besides, it will be nice having a young one around again," she added.

"It isn't like she's a child. She must be in her thirties at least." Harold worried his wife was getting too attached to her.

"I know. She's probably the same age our Charlie would have been." Hazel agreed somberly.

Ronny was overcome with gratitude when she heard the kind words Hazel spoke about her and wished she had the energy to say so. She didn't know why she felt so safe with them, but she did. Her eyelids grew heavy from the medication and she drifted off to sleep again.

"Honey, we're home, dear, would you like to come in out of the heat?" Harold shook Ronny gently but she barely opened her eyes. "Would you like to try and walk? I know you're pretty weak right now but Dr. Callahan said it would be best if you try and do as much as possible on your own. It will help you get your strength back." Ronny wasn't convinced but Harold continued to reassure her. "Come on, lean on me." He helped her out, keeping one arm around her waist as they walked toward the house.

Hazel went ahead to unlock the front door and stood holding it open for them. "Would you like to have a bath, honey? She offered.

"That's very kind of you." Ronny readily accepted the invitation to bathe in a real tub with running water and looked forward to using a plumbed toilet that sat within the house and not without.

"Well, you must be feeling better. That's the most you've said since we met. I'll take her from here, Harold." Harold handed her off to his wife. "I bet we'll find everything you need upstairs in our boy, Charlie's, room." Hazel steadied Ronny by the elbow, as they climbed the long staircase and entered a large bedroom. The walls were the color of eggshells and a red, green and blue plaid spread covered the bed, matching the long curtains that barely skimmed the floor.

"The bathroom is right through here." Hazel pointed to an open door at the other end of the room. "Come on, I'll show you where everything is."

"It's been so long since I've..." Ronny stopped talking, worried her new friend wouldn't approve of her recent past.

Hazel wished Ronny would open up to her but didn't want to pressure her, hoping she would eventually come to trust them enough to speak honestly. "All right then, the towels and washcloths are under the sink and you'll find toothbrushes still in their boxes in that top drawer. I'll come and check on you in a little while and we'll find you some clean clothes to put on, OK?" Hazel turned the knobs, and the faucet dumped warm water into the tub. "Is there anything else I can help you with?"

Ronny smiled weakly. "No, I can't imagine what else I would need but thank you, ma'am." When Hazel had gone, she removed her old clothes as the room filled with steam. She noticed a green plastic bottle sitting on the marble countertop and the liquid bubbles she poured from it, smelled like Irish Spring. When she stepped into the porcelain tub her chafed, chigger-bitten skin itched fiercely as her blood raced from the heat. More shampoo spilled from the bottle than she really needed but she felt luxurious when the white lather formed a bubbly cap on her head. She grimaced at how snarled her hair was and slid under the water. Her mind began to clear a little as she allowed herself to relax and almost fell asleep as she soaked.

Now this is what I call a baptism, she chuckled and it occurred to her how long it had been since she had felt so good. The image of her father's inanimate body lying on the dirt floor of the shack suddenly hung clearly before her. She felt she had the weight of a boulder on her chest and she sat up quickly, gasping for air. "What have I done?" Feeling ashamed she grabbed the washcloth and scoured her body crimson.

"Are you all right, honey?" Hazel asked, rushing into the room.

Ronny hid her face in the warm cloth, sobbing uncontrollably. Without another word, Hazel unfolded a bath towel she took from under the sink and helped Ronny out of the water that had cooled to tepid before wrapping her up and hugging her close. "I heard you holler honey, what can I do to help?"

Ronny felt embarrassed. "I'm so sorry. I must have fallen asleep and had a bad dream or something."

Hazel knew she wasn't ready to talk about it. "It's all right. I just want you to know we're here for you, OK?" Ronny nodded her head.

"Listen, I'll just bet you're not the kind of girl who was made to wear dresses. Am I right?" Hazel grinned.

Ronny was grateful she had changed the subject.

"No, ma'am, I mean yes, ma'am, I *am* the kind of girl who does *not* like wearing dresses."

They laughed together for the first time. "Well, I thought not. I think you'd like some of our Charlie's old things. He kept his clothes starched and ironed, real neat and tidy. Come and take a look." Hazel opened the large closet doors, revealing men's blue jeans and long-sleeved button-down shirts in many soft colors. They were smaller in size than a grown man's, and much more, narrow in the hips and waist than the ones Ronny had been wearing. "Choose anything you want. Do you like these clothes, honey?" Hazel asked sweetly.

"Do, I ever," Ronny whispered, as she ran her fingers along the sleeve of a yellow cotton shirt.

Hazel's heart was full, knowing instinctively they needed one another. "Good. Now you just come downstairs when you're ready and we'll have some supper together, if you feel like doing so. Don't forget to put that cream all over your body before you get dressed. It'll make your skin feel so much better." Hazel pointed to the tube of hydrocortisone she had laid on the bed then turned to leave.

"Miss Hazel?" Ronny stopped her.

She turned to face her guest. "Yes, honey?"

"I don't know how to thank you." Words seemed so small after all the Montgomery's had done.

"We are just so glad to have you here." Hazel squeezed Ronny's hand then left the room to give her some privacy.

Ronny rubbed the cream into her blotchy red skin, then returned to the bathroom to finish getting cleaned up. She noticed the lush bath towels were monogrammed with the upper case letters, **C.D.M.** and speculated the **C** must stand for Charlie. *Where is Hazel's son now?* Ronny brushed her teeth, deciding she would ask about him when she went down to dinner.

A pair of scissors was lying in the drawer next to a box of dental floss and her mind flashed back to Manson always grabbing her by the hair. *Time for a change,* Ronny severed her tangled locks into a bob style then ran a wide-toothed comb through the ends. The coils sprung to life, helping to make her feel a little more human than before. The lines on her face and dark circles around her eyes startled her when she checked her reflection in the mirror. *Who the hell am I?*

She tucked her hair behind her ears and returned to the vast bedroom to get dressed, deciding on a blue chambray, to go with the dark navy jeans that looked almost new. When she slid a brown, braided belt through the loops, she was disappointed to find it needed a few more notches, or she needed to gain a lot more weight before it would fit snugly around her emaciated figure. She hung the belt back where she found it, making do by tying the tails of the oversized shirt into a knot at her waist that was loose enough to modestly cover her torso.

Ronny felt oddly at home as she left the bedroom, skimming her hand over the polished oak banister as she descended the stairs. She was so weak, but hopeful the worst of her life was behind her.

In the kitchen, Harold was rubbing dirt off a bright orange carrot, while Hazel sliced beefsteak tomatoes, fresh from their garden. Ronny had never seen a husband and wife work side by side in the kitchen before. Harold turned when he heard the soft footsteps behind them. "Well hello, child, you look squeaky clean and beautiful. Hazel, look at that fancy new hairdo."

"Well just look at your new cut. It's wonderful, honey. I didn't realize you were a hair stylist," Hazel remarked. Ronny couldn't help but blush at all the attention they were giving her. "I'm not. I just took a chance, that's all. You really think it looks OK?"

"Absolutely, you obviously have a gift," Hazel affirmed genuinely. Ronny considered the notion of being *gifted* at something and her heart skipped a beat.

Hazel carried the plate of tomatoes to the table. "Now you just sit right down here, and let us serve you some good home cooking and tomorrow night you and I can make something together if you'd like."

Harold glanced discreetly at Hazel as the words hung in the air. "Why don't we wait and see if she has made other plans, dear?" Harold suggested.

"Well for goodness sake, Harold." She wiped her hands on her apron then pulled the bench that was really a log sliced in half, out from under the matching solid oak table.

"I'm just saying, maybe we should sit down to dinner and talk a bit before we go putting the cart before the horse." Harold forced a chuckle, but worried his wife was getting her hopes set too high on a girl she knew nothing about.

"Yes, dear, you are right." Hazel sat directly across from Ronny, so they could visit comfortably.

Ronny noticed the couple laying their napkins in their laps and she followed suit, no longer certain of what good manners looked like after being raised by rats.

Her tummy grumbled as her long-lost appetite rose to the surface and her mouth watered at the mere thought of eating the baked chicken and fresh green salad in front of her.

Once they had filled their plates Hazel said, "We noticed a car sitting on the side of the road when we found you, honey. Maybe it was yours?"

Ronny looked down at her plate and picked at her food, obviously wanting to avoid the subject but Harold pressed on cautiously. "I called to have that heap towed while you were getting cleaned up. They called back to say they found it stuck in a ditch farther down the road than where we had seen it." He stabbed a forkful of dark green lettuce.

Ronny couldn't imagine the old lemon would even start again. "I don't understand. Who would have put it in a ditch?"

"Probably someone who wanted to steal it, but they didn't get too far. Anyway, it isn't your problem anymore. It's probably sitting in the junkyard by now," Harold decided.

Ronny sat quietly, thinking how in such a short amount of time, she felt her past belonged to someone else.

"All right now, let's change the subject to something more interesting than all of this car nonsense. About what I said earlier, I got a little ahead of myself and just assumed you would want to stay a little longer than dinner tonight. The truth is, I get the feeling you have nowhere else to go. Harold and I talked it over and we want you to know you can stay here as long as it takes to get you back on your feet."

Ronny wanted nothing more than to get home to Blue, but she couldn't stand the thought of her seeing her the way she was. She needed time to get her strength back first. "I would love to, but what about your son? How does he feel about it? I mean, me wearing his clothes and using his bedroom and all?"

"Our Charlie Dean died years ago, honey. He would have been thirty-one years old this October but he was killed in a car accident when he first started learning how to drive," Hazel explained.

"I'm so sorry. I had no way of knowing." Ronny tried to apologize but didn't know what else to say.

"Of course you didn't, honey, besides, we like talking about our boy as much as we possibly can. It keeps him alive, you know?" Hazel admitted.

Ronny was quiet, taking a moment to think. "Truth is I do need some time to get back on my feet before I head back home to Stockton."

"You live as nearby as Stockton?" Hazel sounded surprised.

Harold took Ronny's hand in his and gave it a gentle squeeze. "We would be delighted to have you stay here with us just as long as you need to. Right now we need to work on getting some meat onto your bones."

Ronny couldn't help but wonder at his genuine concern for her and an unexpected tear rolled down her cheek, as she realized she was in the company of angels.

* * *

SIX

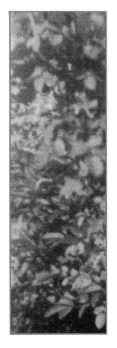

Eva woke the day after her birthday party, to the sun blazing through the bedroom window and her face sticking to her pillow with the heat proving she had slept much later than she had intended. Memories of the previous day brought a smile to her face but were quickly shattered when Sanford called from the hallway.

"Eva! Eva girl! Time to wake up and shine now! We lost a cow last night and you're going to have to go and fetch her back home!"

"What? But I just woke up, Daddy! Why can't Sissy go and catch that stupid cow?" she protested. Sanford tapped gently at her bedroom door. "Come on in," she groaned.

"Well here's the thing about it, girl of mine. We'll be down by the barn picking berries and we both know you don't want that job, so I'm letting you off the hook. You get to go fetch Bessie home instead. You can thank me later." He winked at her.

"What about church?" Eva whined, not really wanting to go but she would much rather that, than mess with a lost cow.

"No church today. We've got too much to do. You know where to find us when you get back, darling." He put his hat on and shuffled down the hallway, whistling a tune.

Although she wished he would take pity on her, Eva was encouraged by his happy mood, considering what had happened the day before. Belle had tried to hide her distress but they had all heard her wailing from the bathroom and tried to pretend they hadn't, when she returned to the dining room with puffy, bloodshot eyes and no explanation.

Eva dressed in her father's long-sleeve shirt and faded blue overalls with holes in the knees, wondering if she was being punished for all the complaining she had done about having to pick berries every year. "Shoot! Why can't I keep my big mouth shut?" she swore, as she put on her tattered leather hat, grabbing a biscuit on her way to the door.

Sanford had left the bucket on the porch that held the kerosene-soaked rags they used for repelling tics and chiggers and Eva sat to tie one odiferous repellent around each ankle. "The last thing I need today is a mess of chiggers in my drawers." She spent most of her efforts feeling sorry for herself as she watched the rest of her family walk down the trail, carrying the familiar white plastic pails. For a moment she thought she might actually miss being a part of the tradition.

She grabbed a rope from the side of the house and headed up into the trees, walking for what seemed forever before she saw a large figure trudging aimlessly toward her. Readying her noose she hollered, "There you are, you old heifer!"

"Whoa now, boy, what do you mean, *old heifer?*" A male voice hollered back at her.

Eva was taken by surprise and she couldn't make up her mind whether to run, or whip him with her rope. She decided to play it tough and yelled again at the approaching figure. "Don't come, no closer, I'm warning you now!"

A handsome young man wearing tan-colored overalls drew near and she could clearly see he was not her beloved Bessie. "Listen, son, I don't mean you any harm, I was just taking a walk through the woods here and..." the unfamiliar voice continued.

Eva interrupted him. "Who are you and what do you want? And who are you calling son?" she demanded of the tall, brown-eyed, white-skinned boy.

"What do you mean, what do I want? I don't want anything like I tried telling you just now, I was looking the place over because my ma and I just moved into town," he pleaded his case.

"You're awful far from town. What brings you out this way in particular?" Eva badgered the stranger suspiciously.

"I discovered a trail that starts at the edge of our backyard and wanted to see where it would take me. Can't a man look around these parts if he takes a notion to do so?" He rubbed his forehead, inspecting the young girl in boy's clothing more closely and laughed out loud. "Why, you're just a little girly beneath that big old hat of yours," he teased her.

Eva grew exceedingly hot under the collar, so she commented sweet and sour as a lemon drop candy, "Who are you calling girly, and more to it, who are you calling a man? I don't see no, man around here."

He stood gaping at the quarrelsome girl, as he had never encountered anyone such as her in all his life. "Well you called me a cow so I guess we're even." He chuckled at his own attempt at humor.

Eva glared at him and stood with both hands on her hips and her chin thrust forward, just daring him to make another mistake with his words as she struggled not to laugh.

He walked a circle around her, rubbing his chin dramatically. "Oh, come on now. You're dressed in boys', coveralls, a man's shirt, rags tied around your ankles, and I'm supposed to know you're a girl?"

Eva remained stubborn as she noticed his light skin that reminded her of milk, and caused her belly to flip-flop. The feeling was something new to her and she wasn't sure she liked it much, so she punched him on the arm with her tiny fist.

"What the...? Are you crazy or something?" He was stunned by her boldness but the sound of a bell clanging distracted him.

Eva was relieved to see her cow bumbling toward them and hoped the boy wouldn't kill her for attacking him the way she did.

"Well, I'm just truly sorry for pounding on you just now but you scared me to death and I tend to react that way when I feel threatened. Uh, I'll just be getting my cow and going on home now if you don't mind." She stammered humbly, rushing past him.

"What? That's *your* cow?" He wanted to prolong her discomfort.

"Uh huh, she's the reason I came out here to the woods dressed like this. She likes to get out and wander from time to time so here I am not, wanting any trouble, just trying to get my cow home." She hoped he would disregard the entire incident.

"Well, by all means, go get your cow." He stepped aside and bowed at the waist, opening one arm wide as if welcoming her down the red carpet.

The rope cut into her hand from gripping it so tightly during the scuffle with the infuriating boy who made her head swim. Ignoring the pain, she swung the cord in a perfect circle above her head, flung it toward Bessie and swore when it hit the dirt again and again.

"Dang you, Bessie, come here!" Eva scolded under her breath, embarrassed she had so little control over the docile beast.

"Are you needing some help there?" the male voice nettled her from behind.

"No, no I've got it. I always do." Eva tried to sound calm even though she was livid she had missed the target so many times.

"Are you sure? Because I might be willing to get her home for you, if you're willing to apologize for beating me up just now," he continued to goad her.

"I do *not* need any help with my own cow." Eva struggled to keep her temper under control. "But thank you just the same."

"I'm thinking maybe your Bessie won't come to you, because you stink something fierce is all." He wrinkled his nose, sniffing the air with exaggeration.

"*Oooh,* I have had it with your insulting ways and I suggest you get on the path you were going down before we met," Eva ordered him, refusing to be manipulated.

"Hold on now, I'm just having a little fun. Besides, the path I was going *down* is the same one you, were coming *up.*" He reminded her. "Listen, I really do want to help. Now what can I do?"

Eva was suspicious but she gave in anyway. "You mean it, because I'm thinking maybe you're right about me stinking like kerosene. I guess I wouldn't want to come near me neither." They called a truce and Eva gave the rope over to him. "Could you give it a try?"

"I would be happy to. I told you so and I meant it." He walked cautiously toward the cow. "Come on now, Bessie. Don't you think you've been enough trouble for one day?"

Bessie seemed to understand and stood still, allowing him to put the rope over her head. He adjusted the noose just tight enough to keep her from slipping away but loose enough for her to breathe easily. Eva was peeved he had captured her with such ease, but his large muscles took her breath away, so she decided to forgive him.

"Now, can I walk her home for you?" he offered sincerely.

Eva opened her mouth to protest but he held up his hand to stop her. "Now wait, I know you can do it all by yourself but I just want to do it, because I want to do it." He tried to convince her.

Eva shut her mouth, realizing she didn't want him to go and would be happy to have his company for the journey home. "All right then, long as you aren't doing it, because you think I can't, because I can," she added firmly.

"Now, didn't I just say that?" He smiled.

They laughed together, easing the tension between them and Bessie groaned loudly as she followed them both down the trail.

"So, you say you moved into old Mr. Henry's place, huh?" Eva tried to make conversation.

He shrugged his shoulders. "Maybe, I don't know who lived in it before us." He was glad to have something ordinary to talk about without the risk of another dispute.

"It's the only one I know to be sitting empty. You know, folks around here thought it would never sell after what happened there." Eva tried to sound mysterious.

"Why? What happened there?" He was suddenly interested in hearing more about the history of his new home.

"Never mind, I, shouldn't have said anything. Weird things start happening when people bring it up," she whispered. "But you're living there now, so you'll be finding out soon enough if the rumors are true." She sought her revenge.

"You're just making up stories to get back at me for all the harassing I did you back there," he tested her, hoping she would admit it was only a joke.

She raised her eyebrows, refusing to commit one way or the other and his imagination ran wild.

Soon they were walking past the house and toward the barn where Eva ran ahead to open the corral gate for the slow-moving animal. Bessie sauntered in, chewing the cud she had ripped from the path as her fellow bovine came to greet her.

Eva closed the gate and turned to face her new friend as he wiped the sweat from his forehead with the sleeve of his shirt. "Thanks for helping me today. I really am glad you came along when you did," she smiled.

Her kind words caught him off guard. "Oh uh, you're welcome. Besides, I haven't been attacked like that since I was a boy wrestling my foster brothers. Felt like old times." He chuckled, baiting her to reply with something equally clever.

Eva wondered what he meant by foster brothers, but thought twice about asking him and took his hand into hers noticing it was most large and strong, by the way.

"Daddy, Mama! Sissy! Come and meet our new neighbor boy!" She pulled him behind the barn where they found them picking blackberries from the half-full bushes. "Mama, Daddy, this here's our new neighbor who just moved into town. Um, uh, well just what is your name anyhow?" Eva giggled.

"Are you going to be clutching at him all day, girl?" Sanford said, straining an attempt at humor.

The young man wiped his damp palm on his pant leg before offering it to Eva's father. "Howdy, Mr. Johnson, what a nice surprise this is."

Sanford shook his hand. "Howdy, Joe, yes sir, this is a surprise. This here's my wife Belle, and our younger daughter, Sissy. I see you already met our Eva," he added deliberately.

"Nice to meet you Mrs. Johnson, Sissy." He nodded politely.

Eva couldn't believe the unlikely coincidence. "What? You two already know each other?"

"Joe's the reason I get to spend more time at home these days," Sanford explained.

"You mean he's the ox? I mean, *boy* Mr. Farnsworth hired?" She tried to understand.

"Yes, sugar, he is." Sanford enjoyed her baffled expression.

"Ox," Joe asked curiously.

Eva was so embarrassed.

Belle stepped forward. "Nice to, meet you, Joe. You're just new to town, then?"

"Yes, ma'am, my ma and I just moved into the house up over the hill there." He thumbed over his shoulder.

Eva noticed Sissy staring at their guest.

"You walked quite a stretch there if you came all the way in from town." Sanford liked Joe, but he was the first boy Eva had ever brought home and he was a *white* boy no less.

"I suppose so, but I guess I'm a lot like Bessie." Joe grinned. "That is, I like to get out and wander around. See what I might have otherwise missed."

Sanford didn't know if he was ready to accept the fact that Eva was old enough to be swayed by handsome young men.

Belle cleaned her sticky hands on her white but purple-stained apron. "You'll be staying for some lemonade, now, won't you, Joe?" She looked tired.

"Thank you, ma'am, but I best be, heading home before Ma starts to worrying. I'd like a rain check though, if you don't mind," he responded appreciatively.

"OK, then, once you two settle in a bit, we'll have you both over for supper," Belle invited.

"Yes, ma'am, we'd like that very much. I figure the more friends she makes, the more willing she'll be to make a go of it here," Joe accepted.

"Bring your pole, boy, and we'll cast a few into the lake," Sanford added.

"We'll look forward to it." he nodded his head to Belle, and shook Sanford's hand again.

"Thank you for helping Eva, fetch our cow home," Belle added warmly.

Joe smiled broadly at Eva in a way that let her know he couldn't wait to see her again. "It was my pleasure."

Eva's mocha skin turned the color of strawberries. "Bye, Joe, hope I didn't hurt you none," she flirted.

He rubbed his shoulder where she had struck him earlier with an exaggerated wince, making Eva giggle again. Sanford wasn't comfortable watching his daughter share a private joke with any boy. "Uh hum!" He cleared his throat. "Need a ride home, Joe?"

"No thank you, sir, just the same." Joe waved goodbye and headed up the hill.

Eva found it impossible to take her eyes off of him.

"You best get in the house and take a Lysol bath, Eva girl." Sanford tried to get her attention but she wasn't quite ready to come back down to earth.

* * *

SEVEN

Eva's head was full of a boy and her belly full of frogs, as she walked around the lake toward the home of her mother's dearest friends. Rosemary Clooney was singing "Mambo Italia no" from inside the red brick house with the Scarlett O'Hara's and moonflowers pervading the entire front entrance. She climbed the stairs and knocked loudly on the screen door hoping to be heard over the music.

"Be right with you!" a voice hollered from inside.

A husky German-born, Missouri-bred woman wearing blue jeans and a white cotton T-shirt appeared from the side of the house. Her dark but graying hair snaked down her back in one long braid and her face brightened at the sight of Eva waiting on the porch. "Oh dear lord! Zoey, come out here! It's our Eva girl come to visit!" She sprinted up the steps and hugged her tightly, then held her at arm's length to look her over from head to toe.

"Hey, Miss Billy." Eva greeted her.

The screen door flew open revealing a thinner, shorter woman with loose auburn curls and ivory skin that looked moist with dew. "Well, Eva child, is it really you? Can't be! When did you walk into womanhood, darling?" Zoey exclaimed excitedly before taking her turn at hugging the daughter of their old friend, Belle.

"I think maybe you're *running* into womanhood, girl. Slow down and let us two old birds catch a breath before you go growing up too fast now." Billy could see Eva enjoyed being teased about getting older.

"Come in and have a seat, baby. It's hotter than Hades out here." Zoey ushered her through the door.

"I've been pulling weeds, so I'll be in as soon as I knock some of this dirt off of me." Billy returned to the bottom step to remove her muddy clogs.

When Eva entered the house, she noticed the neatly arranged jars of pickled watermelon, peaches, and green beans sitting on the counter. Zoey turned down the volume on the stereo.

"I brought you something." Eva handed a white sheet of paper to her before sitting down.

Zoey accepted it graciously and admired the charcoal landscape. "Why, it's just beautiful, dumpling."

"I drew that for you on my birthday," Eva said proudly.

Billy entered the house and scrubbed the dirt from her fingernails at the kitchen sink with a small plastic brush and Lava soap. "Let me see that. Girl, you're getting better and better at your craft. Isn't she, Zoe? We'll frame it and hang it in the living room."

Zoey nodded her head in agreement. "You've come at the right time, pumpkin. I was just finishing up the last batch of spiced peaches." She slipped each hand into oversized oven mitts made to look like chickens then carefully removed the heavy lid from the pressure cooker.

Eva got comfortable at the kitchen table and watched the steam spit and hiss from the steel gray pot. "It's heating up real fast out there." She mopped her brow with a paper napkin she took from the cocky metal rooster posing next to her and held her face in front of the oscillating fan that was blowing from one corner of the room.

"Billy woman, would you get our Eva a glass of sweet tea and some cookies from the crock?" Zoey used wide tongs to extract the hot glass jars from the pot of boiling water, setting them carefully onto a thick towel so as not to scorch the counter top.

"Be glad to, Zoe," Billy replied.

Eva was intrigued as she watched Billy pour the syrupy brew from the gallon jug over ice cubes and mint leaves she picked from the plant on the windowsill. She couldn't help but think how exotic and sophisticated putting mint leaves into a glass of tea was.

"Zoe says mint's good for the stomach." Billy winked. "Here, sugar. Drink this." She handed her the glass and Eva gulped every last bit of the tea willing to suffer through the self inflicted brain freeze.

"I'll be done with this mess in just a few." Zoey tapped each brass lid, making sure they were concave and not convex.

"Well I guess your mama told you we called the other day? She said you, were all just about to sit down to breakfast, so we decided we'd wait and wish you happy birthday next time we saw you." Billy said.

"Yep, I was sitting on the porch with Daddy when the phone rang but she told me you called when we came in to eat." She wiped her mouth with a napkin.

Billy flipped back the red combed head of a rooster shaped cookie jar and Eva jumped when it shrieked an ear piercing crow. "Oh, sorry about that, baby, isn't it just annoying? Zoey says it's supposed to keep us from eating so many cookies but as you can see, it's not working so well." Billy laughed and rubbed her belly. "Anyhow, what's going on with your mama these days, child? She sounded so tired over the phone but promised me she was fine when I asked how she was doing." Billy filled a platter with chocolate chip cookies.

"I don't really think she's doing too well lately, Miss Billy. She locked herself in the bathroom when we were all having a good time at my party, then came out pretending like nothing was wrong even though we all heard her crying. That's not the only time she's done that lately, neither," Eva remarked candidly.

"Hmm, she was never that private when we were all growing up together, that's for sure. She used to be so bold and outspoken. You take after your mama. You know that, sugar?" Billy observed.

"Me? Why I don't see anything of me in my mama. I always wished I did but I don't even look like her," Eva disagreed.

Zoey hoped to soothe Eva's obvious frustration. "You look more like your daddy instead. That's all, baby. This might be a good time to give Eva her birthday present. Don't you think so, Bill?"

"You're right, Zoe. I'll get it from the bedroom." Billy hurried down the hallway, returning in an instant with a package wrapped in plain brown paper and a pink hair ribbon tied in a bow. "Here, pudding." Billy handed it to Eva and took a seat across from her. "Take a break, Zoe."

"I'm coming, I'm coming." Zoey sang, in her naturally cheerful tone. She plopped the pillowy mitts onto the counter and hurried to join the other two. "Wait just a minute now I've got to get the Polaroid!" She reached into a black bag hanging off the back of Eva's chair and pulled out the bulky white camera then raised it to her cheek, closing one eye, hoping to catch the expression on Eva's face. "Well open it, child, we can't stand it any longer." Zoey giggled.

"That's right. It's not going to open itself, you know?" Billy teased.

Eva tugged both ends of the ribbon at the same time then tore away the paper. Inside, was a red vinyl book and she opened it slowly when she realized it was an album full of photographs of Belle and her friends when they were kids.

FLASH! Brilliant, white light temporarily blinded them when Zoey pressed the plastic red button on the side of the camera. They rubbed the spots from their eyes as the photograph slid from the awkward contraption and Zoey quickly swiped the gooey, pink foam cylinder over its surface before laying it carefully on the table. Although they had witnessed this phenomenon a hundred times before, it still fascinated them to see the cloudy, opaque image morph into a vibrant, colorful memento.

"We realize how much you've always wanted to know what your mama was like when she was young, so we dug through some boxes in the attic and found these mixed in with a heap of others from a long time ago when we were all in school," Zoey explained.

Eva looked carefully at each photo and pointed to one of a young girl about twelve years old wearing tan clam digger-style pants and a red short-sleeved shirt, cuffed just below the shoulders. "Oh my, gosh is this Mama?"

"Yes, baby, it is," Billy replied softly, understanding how special this was to her.

Eva noticed the casual way Belle dressed when she was young compared to the formal, old-fashioned way she dressed as an adult. "I've never seen Mama wearing pants before."

"Your mama used to wear nothing but, child. Isn't that right, Zoe?" Billy recalled affectionately. "Yeah, girl, outside of church she didn't wear anything but britches and T-shirts, drove her parents wild!"

Eva glided her hand gently over the slick page, as if she were able to feel her mother's past. "I've wanted something like this always and you two are the only ones who could possibly know how much this means to me." She gave each woman a hug and a kiss on the cheek.

Billy yanked a handkerchief from her back pocket to wipe the damp from her eyes before blowing her nose hard, honking like a goose.

"Well now, sweetheart, let's all get comfy in the living room so we can look at the pictures together. Ooh the memories that came up for the two of us when we were going through those boxes," Zoey said, shaking her head.

"It's true, isn't it, darling?" Billy agreed folding the rag and stuffing it back into her pocket.

"Can I do anything to help?" Eva asked when she noticed Zoey filling two more glasses with ice and setting them with the platter of cookies onto a tray.

"Oh no, sweetheart, you just go on in, Billy and me will, be right behind you." Zoey replied.

Eva sat on the sofa, gazing out the unusually large window. The breathtaking landscape of the clear blue lake and fruit trees that grew just beyond the jumbled vegetable garden was hypnotizing.

Billy entered, and set the tray on the coffee table before taking a seat beside Eva. "Beautiful, isn't it? See the garden there? That's how my parents and their parents planted vegetables in Germany, way back in the day. All scattered about, instead of neat and tidy rows like most folks around here do. Those tin cans laid all in a row, guide the water where it will do the most good to avoid wasting it," Billy explained, as Zoey sat down next to her.

"OK, now let's see some more pictures!" Zoey exclaimed.

Eva opened the book to a random page somewhere in the middle and noticed two teenage girls holding baseball bats and wearing white shorts with navy blue and white striped tank tops. They were smiling and each had her arm around the other. "Who's this standing next to Mama?" Eva was even more curious than before.

Zoey seemed surprised she didn't recognize the girl. "Don't you know who that is? Why, she was your mama's very best friend, Ronny Jean Lawson. Doesn't she ever speak of her?"

"No, I've never heard her name before." Eva felt as if she was learning about the life of a stranger when she saw the unfamiliar girl and Belle posing so intimately. "I didn't know Mama ever played baseball." She decided not to ask what she really wanted to know.

Zoey spoke up. "Oh yes, your mama used to play in all the sports. Isn't that right, Billy girl?"

"Absolutely, if there was a sign-up sheet, your mama and Ronny's names were on it," Billy confirmed.

"Yes sir-ee, those two did just everything together. We were all good friends, of course, but she and Ronny had something real special between them," Zoey recalled, pouring them each a fresh glass of tea over the half-melted ice.

"If they were so close, how come Mama never talks about her?" Eva wondered out loud.

Zoey looked at Billy for the green light to go ahead and speak further on the subject but Billy cleared her throat and continued the story, afraid Zoey might give away too much, too fast. "We don't know about that, but could be it's still just too painful a memory for your mama to talk about."

"Why? Whatever happened to Ronny Jean?" Eva hoped to make sense of it all.

"We only heard the rumors, of course, but the person you could get a solid answer from, besides your mama, would be your daddy, Sweetheart," Billy suggested.

"How did the rumors go?" Eva asked reluctantly.

"Well however the in-betweens were, the long and the short of it is that Ronny and your mama, were building a tree house one day not too far from the church and Ronny's father, he was a wicked man, you know, came and drug her off. Belle tried to find her but ran out of places to look after a while. Missouri's a mighty big place, you know? Anyhow, it all happened so fast, I don't believe they even had a chance to say goodbye. Ronny just seemed to disappear and Belle hasn't been the same since, tell you the truth." Billy explained compassionately.

"Fact is that's when she pulled away from all of us, started wearing her mother's, old-fashioned dresses and showing up in church every Sunday after all those years of trying so hard to get out of going. We tried to be there for her but she just wasn't ready to talk about it, I suppose. We simply drifted apart, other than a brief phone call from time to time." Zoey paused to take a sip of her tea. "She never did finish building that darn tree house neither. Like the spark was snuffed plumb out of her very soul."

The three sat in silence as they tried to imagine what really happened that day.

"But, it was a few years after that, we heard through the grapevine your mama and daddy had gone to the JOP and got hitched." Billy tried to lighten the mood in the room.

"Now, that was a surprise in itself, on account of him having his eye on Miss Gracie all those years. Seemed only natural they would be the ones to marry." Zoey swiftly shoved a cookie into her mouth, wishing she could stuff her words back in with it.

"What? Who's Gracie?" Eva thought the story was getting more and more confusing.

Billy threw an exasperated look at Zoey. "Well, tick tock pick a lock, Zoe!"

"Oh dear lord, I just dumped the dirt right out of my jaw, didn't I?" Zoey crunched on her cookie, hoping to keep herself from saying anything else she shouldn't.

"It's OK. I just thought we were going to ease into all of this a little more slowly, is all." Billy sighed heavily.

Completely unfazed by the two women's discomfort, Eva continued turning the pages of the album as if she would be able to recognize Sanford's old crush. "Is she in here? Daddy's girlfriend, I mean."

They knew she would never be satisfied until she saw a photo of her, so Billy took the book from Eva's lap and turned a couple of pages toward the back. She took her reading glasses from the end of her nose and used them to point at an image in the upper right corner. "There, that's her. That's Gracie," Billy said simply.

Eva felt a tingle race up and down her spine when she saw the beautiful petite girl with eyes that were green like a cat's and full lips, painted the color of chocolate-covered raisins.

Billy and Zoey gaped at the photo, as if they had just seen Jesus and the energy in the room turned electric. How could they have missed what was suddenly so crystal clear to them both?

"Oh! Isn't she just stunning?" Eva declared with barely a whisper, obviously impressed by the young woman's beauty. "So if Daddy loved her so much, why did he marry Mama?"

Billy and Zoey found themselves wondering the same thing, in light of the new revelation staring up at them from the photograph.

Eva was mesmerized by the beautiful woman with the coffee and cream colored skin that matched her own. "There's something familiar about her, does she live around here?" she asked.

Billy's brow creased, as she tried to recall the exact time line. "Uh, now that I think about it, she and her parents left town about four months before she would have graduated from high school, not too long after this picture was taken."

"Huh. Funny we never thought of that long before now, huh, Bill?" Zoey mumbled, deep in thought.

Billy shook her head frantically back and forth, warning Zoey not to add any more details to the subject for the time being. Zoey laughed nervously, flipping the pages to the front of the album, until she found a yellowed black-and-white photo of Belle when she was about five years old, sitting on top of a huge boulder, wearing a pleated coat with a round collar and mittens to match. Her hair had been ironed into perfect ringlets all over her head.

"Whoo-ee, just, look at that scowl on your mama's face there!" Zoey nudged Eva with her elbow, hoping to change the subject and make her smile.

Billy followed her partner's lead. "Ooh! She was so uncomfortable in all that fluff. She'd run down the steps of the church after meeting and start yanking the bows right out of her hair."

"Yes, that's right, and your grandma used to get so mad she'd holler, "Blue Belle? Belle girl! Don'tcha go pullin' at'cha hair now just 'cause, church is through! We're goin' to the Buhler's' house for potluck supper!'" Zoey imitated Belle's late mother to a tee.

Eva grinned, imagining the grandmother she never knew. When Billy noticed she was starting to relax a little bit, she continued, "Yes sir-ee, her curls were so tight, it's no wonder she was always scowling."

The two women laughed out loud at the sweet memories of their friend they missed so much. "Ooh and wearing those frilly little dresses with the big old bows tied just so, right above her little bubble of a butt." Zoey could see the young Belle in her mind like it was yesterday.

Eva sat quietly as the two women reminisced, finally winding down to a mild chortle. "What's on your mind, hon?" Billy asked, dabbing the tears of laughter from her eyes with her handkerchief.

Eva took a cookie from the platter Zoey offered her. "Well, I feel like I've waited so long to know these things, but the more questions that get answered, the more questions there are that come up behind."

Billy wished she could put all the pieces together for her. "Let me tell you a little secret, baby. You're the one that had the birthday, but your mama's been growing up right along with you. I bet she's just waiting for you to come asking about some of these things."

Eva thought about that for a moment. "Why do I feel like you're holding something back from me?"

Billy contemplated the best way to answer her then took both of Eva's hands into hers. "Because, something has come up that I expect your mama would like to talk to you about personally, if you'll only give her the chance to do so."

Eva was disappointed she couldn't know everything right away. "She's never been willing to talk to me about things before, why would she want to now?"

"Why don't you ask her yourself, baby? Stranger, things have happened." Billy hoped it would mean a positive turning point for Eva and Belle.

Eva hugged the album close to her. "Can I take this home?"

"Of course you can darling. Maybe that book will be what brings you and your mama closer together." Billy smiled.

"How do you mean?" Eva asked.

Billy stroked Eva's hair tenderly. "Well, sweetheart, that book tells a story. You came looking for answers about your mama and look how much you learned about your daddy too. Who knows? Maybe you'll even learn something about Eva along the way."

"Would you like to stay for lunch, doll? We're having cold fried chicken and macaroni salad," Zoey invited her.

"Great idea, Zoe, we're going swimming in the lake to cool off after too. Do join us, darling," Billy added.

Eva drank down the rest of her tea. "I would love to, but cows need feeding and berries need freezing." She gave them each a hug, promising to visit again soon. "I love you both so much."

Zoey handed Eva some cookies wrapped in waxed paper and a jar of peaches to take home and they walked her out to the trail. "We love you too, Eva girl. You've always been like our very own."

"Tell your mama to quit being such a stranger and to give us a call real soon," Billy added, with a kiss on top of her head.

Billy and Zoey stood arm in arm, watching as Eva disappeared around the bend when they heard a car pulling into the drive. They hurried to the front of the house, surprised to see a police car. "Afternoon, ladies," Officer Holloway greeted them, respectfully removing his hat.

"Afternoon, what can we do for you?" Billy stepped forward to offer her hand.

"We're looking for somebody that used to live in these parts. Folks in town say you two know this man's daughter." He held up the mug shot of an unusually fat man. "You ladies know him?"

"We'd know that toothless mug any kind of way. That's a cockroach named Manson. We haven't seen him or his daughter in a long while. Been years, in fact," Billy clarified.

"Huh, well we figure he's come back here. A local fellow gave us his description. Says he picked him up when he saw him thumbing outside of town and let him ride in the back of his truck. Apparently, he got out at a stop sign without so much as a thank you. Anyhow, he figured he better report the incident to us because he says the fellah looked real sick and when he got home, he found blood on a bale of hay. Figures the man was hurt pretty bad. Anyhow, you give us a call if you hear anything, won't you?" He handed Billy the customary business card.

Billy took it from him, her mind was racing. "You can bet we will, Officer, he hasn't hurt, anymore kids, has he?"

"Well, I'm not at liberty..." he began, but Billy interrupted him.

Billy hated when people didn't just tell it like it was. "Yeah, yeah, I know. Not at liberty to say. We'll give you a call if we hear anything," she promised.

"You ladies be careful, he's not one you'd ever want to rumble with." He tipped his hat and said good-bye.

"Don't we know it," Billy mumbled, deep in thought.

"What in the world is going on?" Zoey cried.

Billy rubbed her chin, considering the possibilities. "I don't know, Zoe, but if Manson is back in town, our Ronny can't be too far behind."

***

EIGHT

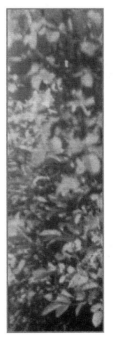

Ronny slept soundly upstairs, while the Montgomery's relaxed in their recliners, sipping their morning coffee, watching the early news on the television. Manson's mug shot and a picture of his car showed on the screen. "Harold! Isn't that the car we saw the day we found Ronny?" Hazel exclaimed.

"...*the driver's seat was covered in blood and the car may belong to this man. If anyone has any information regarding this story, please call your local police station,*" the blonde newscaster announced.

"It is Hazel and I'll bet that's the man who hurt her too." Harold turned it off when he heard Ronny coming down the stairs.

"Well, we know the blood isn't hers, thank God," Hazel said with a sigh of relief. Harold shushed her.

"Morning, sorry I slept so late," Ronny greeted them, looking refreshed and softer around the edges than she had when she first arrived.

Hazel turned quickly at the sound of Ronny's voice. "Well, honey, getting so much good rest certainly agrees with you. You look radiant this morning."

She smiled, and blushed a little less vibrantly at the compliment than she would have only a week ago. She was growing accustomed to being spoken to with such loving kindness. "Want some breakfast before I go out to the woodshed, child?" Harold offered.

"I'll get it, Harold. You go on out and enjoy yourself." Hazel kissed him on the cheek as he put on a hat and headed out the back door. "Would you like some tea, honey? Harold made an especially good brew this morning, if you would care for some."

Ronny followed Hazel into the kitchen and sat down at the table. "Yes, I would, thank you."

Hazel put a stack of warm wheat cakes and a jar of molasses in front of her. "I was wondering if there is something in particular you like to do? I mean in the way of something like my painting and Harold's wood working." She poured hot Constant Comment from the pot, into a large beaker.

Ronny thought for a moment while Hazel added a silver butter plate and knife to the table. "Oh, I've never done anything like that." She breathed in the scent of spiced oranges and cinnamon, thinking she had never smelled anything so good.

"Everyone has a creative side. Maybe you just haven't found yours yet. Would you like to come out to the shed with me, and try something new today?" Hazel invited her enthusiastically.

Ronny ate only half of her food and took a sip of her tea. "Sure." She stood to clear her plate.

"You barely touched your breakfast. Don't let me rush you, honey, you need to eat," Hazel urged her.

"Oh, I'm still not used to eating too much all at once. I've never tasted cooking as good as yours is though." She washed her dishes in the sink before stacking them in the drainer to dry.

"OK then, let's head on outside." Hazel started for the door.

"Miss Hazel? Do you think maybe you could show me around the place? I mean, I've been here over two weeks now and the only time I've been outside is to go back and forth to the doctor." Ronny decided to finish her tea and blew on the steam to cool it down.

"Well, of course. I'd love to show you around." She was happy Ronny felt comfortable enough to ask.

When they stepped out the back door, Ronny couldn't help but notice the majestic American flag flapping in the gentle breeze next to a beautiful red barn with large white X's painted on each door. Balking chickens grabbed her attention as they scratched and pecked at the earth, hunting their breakfast of seeds and insects. A whitewashed fence formed a neat and tidy boundary around a wide, open field where several horses with different colored coats ran up to the fence hoping for a handful of oats. The magnificent landscape brought a lump to her throat, although she wasn't exactly certain why.

"It's all just so breathtaking, Miss Hazel. How could I have missed it this whole time I've been here?" Ronny wondered.

Hazel squeezed Ronny's shoulder. "You've been very ill and on so much medication. Now that you're starting to heal, you'll notice a lot of things you never did before."

There was a swing set just to the side of the house shaded by a thriving, flowering dogwood. In every direction Ronny looked, vibrant timber phlox, ferns, and wild geraniums, flourished throughout the yard. "Seems like, everything around here grows healthy and beautiful."

"That's right, young lady, just like you." Hazel hooked her arm with Ronny's and they made their way to the front of the white, two-story colonial-style home. Each window was flanked with black shutters and the flower boxes were spilling over with sweet peas and blue bells. Hazel thought Ronny was about to cry. "Are you all right, honey?"

"Yeah, I'm fine, Miss Hazel," she hedged; wishing Blue was there with her. She noticed a brass plaque above the doorway, with the words "*Salus Populi Suprema Lex Esto*" etched into it. The language seemed peculiar, yet empowering, even though she had no idea what it meant.

"I'm sure I've seen that before, but I never did know what it was saying." She pointed at the engraved ornament.

"It looks familiar to you, because it's Missouri's state motto. It means the wellness of the people shall be the supreme law." Each day spent with Ronny, made Hazel realize just how sheltered she had been.

Ronny contemplated the notion for a moment, as a lifetime of abuse from her own father flashed before her. "Wouldn't that be nice if it were only true?"

Hazel sensed she was more emotional than she had been when she was on her medication. "Come on, let's go back inside. Maybe you would like to lie down for a while?"

"Oh no, I'm fine, Miss Hazel. I feel better than I have in a very long time, thanks to you and Harold. Please, let's go on with what you had planned."

Hazel smiled. "Well, if you're sure. But first I want to show you something." They went back inside the house, and Hazel led her to an area Ronny had not yet seen.

Enchanting abstract paintings hung tastefully on the walls and the polished, mounted wood carvings, clay bowls, and flower vases adorning the nooks and niches created the feeling of being in an art museum.

"Did you make all these things?" Ronny asked, awestruck.

Hazel chuckled. "Well, I didn't make *all* of them. I did the paintings and Harold worked with the wood. Charlie made the pots and bowls and such. We feel it's important that a person find what truly moves them inside. You know something that expresses one's true spirit."

Ronny had never heard such ideas but she knew right away she would like to learn more about anything at all from the fascinating woman with the fancy way of talking.

"Would you like to see what you can do?" Hazel hoped Ronny would say yes.

"Who me, I can't, do anything like this."

"You never know until you try. Would you believe none of us knew how any of these things were going to turn out? Take Charlie's vases here. He had no idea they would look like this. They just sort of came to be these everlasting objects of beauty," Hazel mused.

"Really, I can't imagine," Ronny said.

"Truly, honey. You just have to let go and let your creative spirit take over," Hazel assured her.

"I suppose I could try something." Ronny decided.

"Well all right then. Off we go." Hazel led the way through the backyard and into the barn, swiping her hand through the air to remove the cobwebs hanging from the rafters as they entered. Other than a little dust from lack of use, the space was clean and organized with tools of every kind lining the walls in an orderly way. Sitting in the middle of the smooth concrete floor was an odd-looking contraption with a single stool in front of it. Hazel clapped her hands together, elated to be sharing this moment with Ronny. "There it is. It belonged to our Charlie," she announced.

"What is it?" Ronny felt ignorant.

"It's a potter's wheel. This is what Charlie used to make the things you saw in the house," she explained.

Ronny examined it more closely while Hazel pushed open the stable-style doors to let the sun shine in. "I've never seen one of these before. What do you do with it?" Ronny wrinkled her nose.

The words were music to Hazel's ears. "I'm glad, you asked. Dust it off and we'll make some magic today." She tossed her a cloth and went to the refrigerator to remove a large square of clay wrapped in clear plastic and dumped it onto the cool, stainless steel counter. While Ronny wiped the dust and webs from the wheel, Hazel took the wrap from the clay then sliced the end off with a wire that looked like a guitar string and massaged it until it was warm and pliable. She slapped the heavy lump down hard onto the wheel and Ronny admired how toned her arms were.

"Now, fill this bucket with warm water over at the sink, if you would, please." Hazel handed her a pail and sat at the wheel. When she flipped the switch, the motor started to hum and she pressed her toe down gently on the pedal of the machine. Momentum started to build as she took control of the clay, manipulating it with skill and vigor.

Ronny returned with the full pail and set it on the floor where Hazel could easily dip her hand into it and dribble water onto the mass without skipping a beat of the powerful rhythm beneath her experienced hands.

The mud grew tall and cylindrical, then short and paunchy, depending on which direction the maestro pressed and pulled, as if conducting her orchestra. Ronny was captivated as she witnessed the sensational demonstration. When Hazel lifted her foot from the pedal, the unfinished creation tumbled and collapsed, as if a spell had been broken. She rose from her seat smiling, flushed from the exhilaration that only comes from the anticipation of creating the unknown.

"Now you try it, honey." She offered Ronny the stool.

Ronny was eager to experience that kind of sensation herself and sat down to take possession of the malleable earth. When her foot hit the pedal, the vibration laced with the gritty texture beneath her palms was intoxicating as she molded and shaped without intimidation. Her skin tingled, as raw emotion rose to the surface. Grief and sorrow flooded her soul purging, themselves from her heavy, laden chest. The unidentifiable form, oozed through her knuckles as she clenched her fists, pounding the heap of wet earth, wailing like a coyote cub abandoned by its pack.

Harold heard her and rushed from the shed armed with a carving knife, ready to defend the women in his care but stopped abruptly when he saw they were safe. He wanted to show respect to their woeful houseguest and took a step back.

Ronny grew weak and slid from the stool, onto the floor. Hazel held her close, rocking her gently back and forth like a newborn baby. "I'm sorry! I'm just so very sorry!" Ronny cried.

Hazel dabbed her blotchy red cheeks with a sweet-smelling handkerchief as the tears continued to flow.

"You don't need to be sorry for anything ever again, young lady. Not here not with us," she said, comforting the orphan.

The words flowed easily for the first time and Ronny told the tale of the past fourteen years as Hazel listened with the patience of a true friend and at the same time fumed with protective, motherly wrath. Ronny admitted she was worried the police would arrest her for killing her father, burning down his house, and stealing his car.

"Don't you worry about any of that now, you have Harold and me to shield you from such concerns, but you know what needs to be done, don't you, honey?" Hazel asked carefully, tenderly.

Ronny felt as though her heart had stopped beating. "I'm so afraid, Miss Hazel. Will you help me?"

"Absolutely, we'll be with you every step of the way. Now listen, Dr. Callahan already knows what you've been through. Your body told him that much. We've just been waiting for you to tell us who had done this to you. Now we know and any judge that hears what that devil did could never blame you for the way things turned out. Besides, Harold and I will hire the best damn attorney in all of Missouri to help you."

Something about Hazel always made Ronny feel strong and capable. "You would do that for me?"

"Why, honey, don't you know? We promised to take care of you and that's just what we're going to do." Hazel ran her fingers gently through Ronny's hair.

"Uh hum." Harold cleared his throat. "Hello, ladies, what say we all go inside and have some lemonade?" He tried to sound as if he hadn't witnessed the sorrowful scene, but was unsuccessful at convincing them when he blew his nose into his handkerchief and wiped the water from his eyes.

Ronny clung to Hazel as if she were her only source of security. "I hardly know you but I know I love you, Miss Hazel."

She held Ronny close, as if she were someone she had longed for all of her life. "I love you too, honey, I love you too."

Harold helped the women to their feet putting his arm around his wife and his hand on Ronny's shoulder as they strolled toward the house. One was convinced she had found the parents God intended her to have and the other two felt they had resurrected the son they buried years ago.

* * *

NINE

"Well, who in the world can that be this time of night?" Eunice complained when the doorbell rang. "Who is it?" She prudently clutched her robe at her throat.

"It's me, don't turn on no lights just go get your mother." The reply came deep and portentous.

She recognized the gruff tone immediately, as she had longed for the day when she would hear it again, see him again. She abandoned all modesty and allowed her robe to hang open before turning the deadbolt and yanking the door. "Dear God, I knew you'd come back someday, I just knew it!" she effused, as if she didn't even notice how ripe he smelled.

Eunice Buhler had never left home and never married, waiting for her teenage crush to love her. They had met when she was just a girl, at the military academy she and her parents visited every Sunday after church. They went there to read scriptures and preach the gospel to those who refused to conform to the strict rules and regulations of the school.

"What's going on out there, Eunice," Beatrice screeched from the bedroom.

"Mama, you'll never believe it!" she hollered excitedly. "Come in, come in and have a seat." Eunice invited him and shut the door slowly, scanning the yard as she did hoping someone besides the lightning bugs had noticed her inviting a man into her home, especially so late at night. Once he was seated on the sofa, she hurried into her mother's bedroom.

"You better tie that robe around you, girl, before I knock you from here to kingdom come," The man heard the old woman reprimand her daughter.

Eunice returned fully covered, pushing Beatrice in a wheelchair, and the old woman instantly recognized the outline of the man's large form.

Widow Beatrice was a strict and pious Christian who wore her hair in a severely tight bun. Her husband had been the only preacher in the only church the town had ever known until he died many years ago, but she still considered herself to be the last word in all things concerning the congregation. She was confined to a wheelchair due to her rheumatoid arthritis and she carried the burden of a secret she had tried over and over to hide, but there he was, sitting on her sofa. She greeted him with her usual stone face, completely devoid of emotion except for the barely noticeable flicker in her eyes that hinted of something more personal between them.

"Well, well, well, it really is you. I thought Eunice had lost her mind or seen a ghost. Why are we talking in the dark, girl?" Beatrice held her handkerchief to her nose to fight the stench coming from their guest.

Eunice stepped hastily toward the light switch, but stopped in her tracks when the man snarled, "I told you I don't want, no lights!"

The women were abruptly reminded how dangerous their guest could be, so Eunice did as she was told.

"All right then, no lights." She was wringing her hands, trying to conceal her nettled nerves. "Can I offer you a cup of coffee or some food?" she fussed flagrantly, hoping to please him, needing desperately to be noticed by him.

He blatantly ignored her and grumbled to Beatrice, "I didn't know where else to go."

Beatrice smirked. "You did the right thing by coming here. Where have you been anyhow?"

He lied carefully, forcing every word between each excruciating, shallow breath. "We've been livin' in St. Louis. You know how headstrong the girl's always been. She ran and stole my car, so I came after her. Found it on the highway. No sign of her though, so I figured maybe she came back around these parts."

Beatrice was a shrewd old bird and besides seeing his car and face on the news, she also knew he was a practiced deceiver, so she continued to probe him cautiously. "I'm surprised you took the girl somewhere as big as St Louis. It just isn't like you to go where there's, so many people."

"Ain't, none of your business, woman. Now, I'm gonna need you to stay quiet about me bein' here. Got it?" The warning sounded more like a threat, even though he winced as he spoke, unable to ignore the sharp pain slicing through his body. He pulled a bottle from his belt and chugged homemade whiskey from it until his head spun.

Beatrice knew something was very wrong but she couldn't see just what it was in the dark. He coughed uncontrollably. "Oh, for goodness sake, this is ridiculous. Eunice, turn on that lamp there, so we can see what's going on with him."

Eunice turned the switch on the brass lamp next to the ailing man. They gasped out loud when they saw him shaking like a junkie in his blood soaked clothing and the amount of sweat pouring down his badly charred face.

Eunice rushed to his side when he collapsed with a loud grunt and she touched her hand to his forehead. "Oh you poor, poor baby, what has happened to you? He's burning up, Mama! What shall we do?" she whimpered.

There was no response from the unconscious man who was glutted with infection and almost certain to die.

"Get him a cold cloth and get me the phone." Beatrice ordered coldly.

Eunice handed the telephone to her mother before retreating to the kitchen and Beatrice dialed the home of Reverend Dan Phelps.

"Yes, who is it?" he demanded, angry to be woken up.

"It's Buhler. Our wayward sheep has found his way home and he needs a doctor. That means your wife and she best not say a word about it to anyone, understand?" she warned him.

The reverend looked at his wife snuggled under the blankets sleeping soundly after working a long week at the hospital. "Whoever it is, take them to the clinic. I'm not going to ask Betty to get up and come over there in the middle of the night."

Beatrice looked over each shoulder, making sure her daughter was beyond hearing range. "It's our boy and he's about to die!" she whispered anxiously into the receiver. "You just tell your *precious,* it's one of your flock and you have to help him and keep it a secret. I'm sure she'd do anything to help her *reverend* husband," she sneered, exuding jealousy.

He was speechless for a moment, trying to find his voice. "I can't get her involved in something like this. She has her reputation to protect."

"You should be more worried about your own reputation, if you don't keep doing as I say. Understand, Reverend? Remember, I gave you that title and I can take it away."

He groaned, wishing he hadn't answered the telephone at all. "Understand. Give me a little time to talk to her." He was weary, wondering when he would ever find the backbone to stand up to the obstinate manipulator.

"Good, because if you don't, you know I will," she promised.

When the phone hummed dead, the reverend hung his head, regretting a time long ago when he was a hormonally motivated boy and Buhler was a pretty, older, and promiscuous girl. Poor Eunice had no idea she had been lusting after her own half brother all these years and that the good Reverend Phelps, was Manson's secret daddy.

* * *

TEN

Eunice rushed to answer the door when the Reverend and more importantly, the woman who could save Manson's life, arrived. "He's on the sofa." Beatrice directed Dr. Betty Phelps without sentiment. Even through burned flesh, the doctor recognized the foul-smelling patient as Stockton's long lost child molester. When she noticed the amount of blood loss, the thought occurred to her to try to get out of saving him.

"I can't do anything for him, he's too far gone." She said bluntly.

Beatrice threw Dan a threatening grimace.

"Please, Betty, do what you can," he pleaded with her.

She decided her conscience would haunt her if she didn't at least try to do something. "Damn the Hippocratic oath," she swore under her breath, as she put on rubber gloves then cut the blood-soaked jacket off of him. Betty had seen a lot of trauma in her career, but she almost threw up when she saw the burned rolls of fat and deep stab wounds in his back. "Hold him up Dan." The reverend forced the fat man forward, while the doctor dumped a full bottle of alcohol into the gaping lacerations without the slightest hint of bedside manner. "Get a bucket of hot, soapy water and a sponge with a rough side." She directed Eunice but she just stood there looking puzzled, stupid as to how the doctor planned to use the items. "Go! Unless you want him to die," Betty ordered her.

Eunice scurried to the kitchen and quickly returned with the things she had asked for.

The doctor used the scratchy side of the sponge to scrub the swollen, inflamed injuries until they were free of dirt and pus, then slowly stitched each of the throbbing gullies together with great satisfaction, as the wanted felon fought back the tears. She smeared iodine all over his burned flesh, then wrapped him around and around with white gauze. Once the wounds were cleaned and dressed, she stabbed him with a needle that was barely sharp enough to penetrate the thick layers of adipose. The syringe was full of antibiotic and the only hope of killing the infection surging through his veins.

"That's the best I can do." Thrusting a bottle of penicillin and pain pills at Beatrice, she instructed the old woman, "Six a day of one and whatever's needed of the others." Then turned and glared at her husband who opened his mouth to apologize, but thought better of it when she raised her hand to him, making it perfectly clear she didn't want to hear it. She had no intention of telling him she would be calling the police first thing the next morning.

"Nice lady," Beatrice snubbed the doctor caustically as Dan opened the door his wife had just shut in his face.

"Beatrice..." He wanted to tell her to leave him alone, to stay out of his life but decided she wasn't worth another argument and ran to meet his wife outside, closing the door behind him.

It had been a long time since Beatrice had heard her name fall from those lips and she grimaced when she felt her cold heart skip a beat or two.

* * *

ELEVEN

Eunice had dutifully spent three days and nights looking after Manson. Each day, she crushed the pills before dissolving them in water then lifted his head into her lap so he could drink the healing concoction. She carefully washed his blistering face before applying more ointment and kept him covered with clean blankets. He shivered and vomited bile into a bucket she held under his mouth as his toxic body attempted to save itself.

As she cared for him, she remembered the day her parents had brought him home from the academy. He had spent his first few years of life in an orphanage and when they couldn't manage his behavior, they sent him to the academy as a last resort. Reforming Manson was impossible and Beatrice was haunted by her guilty conscience so she convinced her husband the only hope of saving the boy was to bring him home and raise him with Christian values. No one but she and Dan Phelps had any idea he was their bastard son they had given up the moment he came out of her womb.

Eunice had loved Manson since the first time he came to her bedroom in the middle of the night when she was just a teen. She had mistaken his lust for true love and was devastated when he married Enid. She had wasted her life, pining for him hoping someday he would be hers, but once he found others to fill his needs, he never seemed to notice her again.

After another long night, Eunice showered and dressed before going to the kitchen to make a pot of coffee. She desperately needed sleep but she had to go to the church to teach vacation Bible school. Beatrice was just wheeling herself out from the bedroom when Manson started to wake up. "Eunice, Eunice!" she yelled, uncharacteristically.

Eunice hurried from the kitchen still holding the stack of paper coffee filters. "Oh dear Jesus, it's a miracle!" she gushed, rushing to kneel by his side.

"Where the hell, am I?" he mumbled, still in a daze from the near-death experience.

"You're home, boy. You came here sick and we got you a doctor to make you well again," Beatrice explained dryly, regaining composure.

His head started to clear a bit. "What? I told you I don't want, nobody knowin' I'm here." He was furious at their disobedience.

Beatrice had had her fill of his bad attitude but held her tongue. "And they, won't neither. You don't worry a thing about it. Fact is, you're alive and right now that's all that matters."

Manson struggled to sit up, flopping around like a turtle that had landed on its back held down by his own rotundity. Eunice got behind him and pushed crudely with all of her strength, being careful not to touch his wounds but the sliding rolls of fat made it difficult to keep her hands on target. After several attempts, he sat upright and she hurried to the bathroom to get some clean towels to cover the bloodstained sofa.

"Are you hungry?" she chirped when she returned, unable to keep from staring at his badly burned face.

Manson looked right past her, scowling at Beatrice. "I need to get out of here and take care of my business."

Beatrice eyed him coolly. "We welcomed you into our home in the middle of the night, found a doctor that agreed to keep her mouth shut about ever seeing you, and Eunice here has been long suffering nursing you back to health. The least you can do is, answer the woman when she offers you a sandwich!"

Eunice had never heard her mother speak to him in such a way and she stood rigid, waiting to see what he would do but he only rolled his eyes, feeling fatigued at the very thought of having to placate the infuriating females. "Yes, I'm hungry," he groaned.

Eunice relaxed and bustled happily to the kitchen to fix their ungrateful guest something to eat.

Manson rubbed his chin and flinched when he touched the sagging flesh. "What the hell's goin' on?"

"I take it you haven't looked in a mirror in quite some time? You're burned up real bad, not to mention you've been stabbed in the back, twice." Beatrice was delighted to see him in a vulnerable position.

Manson was swiftly reminded of the day Ronny had left him for dead. The dirt floor had prevented the fire from doing any damage beyond him and the mattress but he remembered choking on the smoke and rolling back and forth to put out the flames that were frying his skin. He could still hear himself scream as he pulled the knife from his back. The adrenaline rush allowed him what he needed to get dressed but it took him three days to stumble the length between the shack and the highway as he grew weaker but more determined not to let Ronny get away with what she had done. He planned to make her pay.

"Manson? Who did it to you?" Beatrice startled him from his daydream as she pushed a little further.

He wasn't about to tell the town crow his own daughter had suckered him, so he ignored the question.

Beatrice eyeballed Eunice when she returned with a bologna sandwich and barbecue potato chips. "Have you seen his girl anywhere around town?"

"No, ma'am, I wouldn't be caught dead in the places she'd go anyhow, I'm sure. Maybe she's hiding at her girly friend's house." Eunice was snide with her remarks, trying to impress the vile man with her self-righteousness.

"Who, Belle?" he sneered.

Beatrice couldn't wait to share the gossip. "Her parents are dead but she's still living out at the lake house, married to Sanford Johnson."

"Is she now? Well, ain't that just a slick way to try and throw folks off her scent?" he scoffed.

"Yeah, who knows what she's really doing when her old man and daughters aren't around," Eunice slandered Belle sanctimoniously.

"Daughters, now that is somethin'. How old are they?" He suddenly decided he needed to take some time outside of looking for Ronny to play a little while he was in town. The mere thought of Belle's daughters made him start to feel better and he took a bite of his sandwich.

Eunice was glad she could finally impress him. "They're still young enough to be in VBS."

"Huh, I guess I've been gone longer than I thought. I'm gonna need a place to stay while I'm here," he hinted, already determined not to leave.

Eunice gave Manson his pills without crushing them, now that he was able to sit up and talk. He chugged them down with water and grew tired again wanting to be left alone so he could sleep.

"We'll make up a bed in the basement for you. You can stay as long as it takes to get your family back together. Speaking of, where's your wife, Enid, anyhow?" Beatrice pried.

Manson held his hand to his heart, his eyes raised toward the ceiling. "She's my dearly *departed* wife now, as I buried her not too long ago. Had a bad fever she did and the doctors was too late to save her," he lied.

A nefarious grin spread across Eunice's face and a twinkle sparked in the aging spinster's eyes as he spoke of Enid's untimely death. "Too bad for you, every man deserves a good Christian woman to serve him in these wicked times." She sniveled with false pity.

"You're looking tired. Why don't you lie down and get some rest," Beatrice said to Manson but glowered at her daughter's obvious flirtatiousness, so Eunice took Manson's plate into the kitchen. "Listen, Manson, you can't just go wandering the streets looking for the girl. The police have the whole town looking for you. You need a plan."

Manson already had a plan in mind as the drugs took their course and he drifted off to sleep, comforted by the thought of his favorite Bible verse. *An eye for an eye...a fire for a fire...a daughter for a daughter...*

* * *

TWELVE

Eva and Sissy ran up the stairs of the newly painted church, giggling like girls their age tend to do. Sissy wrinkled her nose. "Whoo-ee, Eva girl, smell that stinky paint!

"Yeah, I told Preacher Dan they should have painted it any color but boring white but he says white's the color of purity. Of course, I bet he never caught Nelly and Stubbs kissing in the organ room neither." Eva laughed.

Sissy laughed too then covered her mouth as if Eva had said something terrible. "Ooh, you better not let Miss Buhler hear you talking like that or she'll tan your hide."

Eva scoffed, "Oh let her tan me. I don't care. The older I get, the less interested I am with all of it. I mean, I don't know why they call it *vacation* Bible school, as I never do feel I'm on vacation in *any kind* of way when I'm listening to Buhler preach about God killing people just because they done things that made other folks uncomfortable. If that's all it takes to make God mad, I'm in big trouble. I mean, I make folks uncomfortable all the time, so what am I doing sitting in church when I could be anywhere else but, awaiting my imminent demise? No Sissy, I cannot believe the same God who gave us these beautiful bodies and this magnificent earth to enjoy could ever be that vengeful and mean."

Sissy shrugged her shoulders as Eva pulled on the heavy wooden doors. They stepped onto the blood-red carpet that led them across a shadowy corridor, then down a set of narrow cement stairs and into the classroom where several other children Sissy's age sat waiting with an irritated Miss Buhler.

"You girls are late!" she scolded them harshly.

"Yes, Miss Buhler," Eva responded, forcing sincere reverence as she and Sissy took their seats. Eva couldn't help but feel like Alice in Wonderland when she squatted down on a tiny wooden chair intended for children much younger and smaller than herself.

Class resumed with Eunice droning on and on with the religious rhetoric, boring Eva to tears as she illustrated the lesson using jagged felt cutouts that vaguely resembled tiny rigid people wearing long robes, desperately clinging to a fuzzy white board. The impatient Bible teacher struck the table with an old yellowed ruler.

"Miss Johnson! What do you think you're doing, young lady?"

Eva screamed and jumped to attention, struggling to sit up straight. "Nothing, Miss Buhler," All the other students except for Sissy, laughed at Eva's misfortune.

"You're sleeping is what you're doing, missy! Why don't you explain to the rest of the class what I was talking about just now?" Eunice dared her.

Eva glanced quickly at the indistinct felt people and noticed all the men had long hair and beards. "Um, I think you, were talking about, uh Jesus?" She thought her answer was a safe assumption.

Buhler felt smug and reverently patted the tattered black book lying next to her on the table. "No sir-ee, child. I was talking about how nobody but those who live righteously by the good book will be allowed to walk through the pearly gates of Heaven."

All eyes were on Eva as she replied cautiously, but with confidence. "But if we're, all made in God's image, like the Bible says, that makes us all righteous just as we are. Doesn't it?"

Eunice loomed menacingly over her with pursed lips, pointing her ruler threateningly. "Why, you contemptuous little heathen! Come with me." The students were quiet as church mice when Eva stood from her seat feeling just a little bit anxious, wishing Buhler would leave the ruler behind. She followed her teacher upstairs, forced to listen to Eunice admonish her.

"You will not be poisoning the minds of the others that come here to learn God's will like your mama did when she was your age." Eunice heaved the ponderous door open and stood with her back against it, looking down her nose at Eva. "You're lucky we can't get away with smacking you spoiled brats around like my mama did. She used to whack your mama real hard on the knuckles with this very same ruler, and if she didn't make her bleed the first time around, she sure did the next." She spanked her own palm gently with it as she spoke.

Eva's blood ran cold. "Excuse me, Miss Buhler? Are you kidding?"

Eunice blinked and came back to the reality in front of her. "What? Oh, get on out of here before I decide to bend the rules to my liking," she threatened her. Eva stepped out from the air-conditioned church into the blazing heat and Buhler turned on her heel and marched back into the dismal cave.

On one hand, Eva felt the sting of her words, but on the other, wondered why she hadn't come up with a scheme to get kicked out of church a long time ago. While she waited on the steps for Sissy, she wondered what Buhler meant about her mama poisoning the minds of the other students. She tried to imagine her parents as teenagers, talking and playing after church in that very same parking lot with their friends and wondered why her father's old girlfriend Gracie seemed so familiar. She lay upside down on the concrete steps, pretending what was up was down, and what was down was up, and something caught her eye just beyond the parking lot.

"Can't be, after all these years, can it?" Eva felt dizzy when she sat upright and the blood rushed from her head back down to her toes. Once she regained focus, she could see several narrow boards nailed to the trunk of a tree and a large cluster of branches held a half-built house in the palm of its gnarled and knotted hand.

She leaped to the bottom step then sprinted across the parking lot. There was evidence a path once led to the tree, but the overgrown thicket prevented her from getting anywhere near it. She tried to force her way through but the barbs pierced her skin, cutting her arms and legs making it impossible to get past the perilous flora.

"Ow!" Eva yanked her arm back to inspect the stinging wounds. Disappointed, she turned to go when she noticed something on the ground, glistening in the sunlight. She couldn't be sure but she thought it was a silver heart-shaped locket. *How did Mama's necklace get out here?* Her curiosity spiked so she lay on her belly and crawled under the brambles, instead of charging directly through them. Reaching as far as she could, she finally grasped the prize in her hand and was almost giddy as she scooted backward and stood to her feet.

"I always wondered what the big secret was about this old thing." Skimming her finger over the filigree, Eva hesitated, feeling as if she were invading someone's privacy as she ran her thumbnail along the edge until the tiny clasp opened, revealing two small photographs. In one half of the heart, Eva saw a younger version of Belle and her mother's mysterious friend smiled from the other. "The Ronny girl I saw in the, photo album." She gasped.

"What are you doing Eva," Sissy shouted, startling her out of her skin. Eva whirled around to find Sissy standing directly behind her with an interrogating look on her face.

"So help me, Sissy! One of these days," Eva scolded her.

"Sorry. What's going on? Why are you all scraped up and dirty?" Sissy persisted innocently.

Eva dropped the pendant discreetly into the front pocket of her dress. "Never you, mind, let's get on home. Joe's coming for supper again this evening." Eva put her arm around her younger sister and they walked the trail toward home, completely unaware of the drooling fat man, starved for young flesh, watching from the thick of the nearby hazelnut bushes.

* * *

THIRTEEN

Joe wore goggles and leather gloves for protection from the monstrous machine that cut the timber and threw the dust.

Sanford shoved his time card into the mouth of the clock and waved to Joe that it was time for dinner. "Hey, Joe," He hollered, hoping to be heard over the grinding saw.

Joe stopped feeding the hungry device and it wound down to a dull roar. "Hey, Mr. Johnson, I enjoyed having supper with you all last night. Mrs. Johnson sure does make the best pork chops I ever tasted. But don't tell my ma I said so." He winked and held his finger up to his lips as if he had told a secret.

"We were glad to have you. Especially Eva of course, maybe next time, your ma can come along. What say we eat together today, visit a spell?" Sanford wanted to get better acquainted.

"Is it dinnertime already? Whoo-ee! Time does fly when we're having fun, doesn't, it?" He removed his protective garb, shaking the sawdust from his hair as they headed out the door together.

"Why don't you join me on the tail of my truck?" Sanford offered.

"OK, just let me get my food out of the icebox in the break room and I'll meet you outside." He went one direction and Sanford went the other. Sanford was already unpacking the leftover fried chicken Belle had packed for him and sipping an Orange Crush soda pop when Joe joined him on the tailgate and took his turkey sandwich from the wrinkled waxed paper.

"So how are you two getting along, son? Are you settling in all right by now?" Sanford crunched on a potato shoestring.

"Oh yeah, I haven't seen Ma so satisfied before. Fact is she spent so much of her life moving around like she's been searching for something only to end up right back where she started from," Joe mentioned casually.

Sanford's curiosity was piqued. "What's that you say? I thought you all were new to town."

Joe washed down his sandwich with the sweet iced tea he poured from a stainless steel thermos before answering Sanford. "We are, but this is where Ma lived when she was just little. Didn't I mention that the other day?"

Sanford chewed on a cold chicken leg then wiped his greasy fingers on a napkin. "No, Joe, you didn't mention it at all." He set his food aside and slid a cigar from his shirt pocket, cupping his hands around the end to light it. His mind raced with images of friends and foes that had come and gone over the lifetime he had lived there. *Could Joe possibly be Ronny's boy? His skin is certainly as white as hers.* Sanford tried to be discreet as he stared at Joe, looking for any resemblance between him and Belle's true love. He was so excited at the notion, his heart pounded fervently beneath his shirt as he searched for the right words to say.

Joe noticed the sudden change in Sanford. "Something wrong, Mr. Sanford?"

Sanford blew a smoke ring into the air and watched it float away before continuing. "You know, Joe, I've lived in this small town all my life. Very few folks ever moved in or out of here and I could have sworn I knew each and every one of them that did. Wouldn't it be a hoot to find out I knew your ma too?" He was hoping he did.

Joe wrinkled his forehead. "I hadn't thought of that but maybe you do. Does the name Gracie ring a bell?"

Sanford choked on the smoke from his cigar and yanked it from between his teeth, coughing deep from his chest. Water stung his eyes as images of the past flooded his mind.

Joe tossed the last bite of his sandwich onto the ground and pounded Sanford between the shoulder blades, hoping to resuscitate him, while Sanford rocked back and forth, wishing Joe would stop beating on him so he could catch his breath.

"Are you all right, Mr. Johnson? Did I say something wrong?" Joe asked anxiously when he noticed the healthy glow fading quickly from Sanford's cheeks.

"No, no, boy. Just sucked her down the wrong pipe is all," he said wheezing.

Joe checked the time on his wristwatch. "Shouldn't we be getting back?"

"Now don't be in such a toot, son. We've got a few more minutes. I'm thinking it's kind of funny you saying your ma's name, is Gracie." He chuckled nervously.

"Oh, yeah how so," Joe stood from the tailgate and handed Sanford his soda.

"Well now, you're going to laugh at this one. The only Gracie I ever knew from around these parts was a dark colored girl, so I guess we can be pretty sure she's not your ma, huh?" He took a long drink from the bottle.

"My ma's a black woman. Not quite as dark as you but black just the same," Joe commented offhandedly.

Sweat broke out on Sanford's forehead and his mind raced to the past. "I don't know if you noticed this or not but you're white as rice, son!" He laughed unsteadily, meaning no disrespect.

Joe grinned. "Well, you see now, I'm her *adopted* son, so I guess there's a good chance you know her after all. Of course, we'll find out soon enough, huh?"

"Adopted? What? We will?" Sanford's head was spinning and he couldn't make sense of what Joe was saying.

"Well yeah, didn't Mrs. Johnson tell you? She told me to ask Ma if dinner on Sunday after next at your place would be a good time for all of us to get together, so I did, and it is. She can't wait to meet Eva, that's for sure." Joe smiled brightly. "Well, I expect we'd best be getting back to it, huh?"

Sanford went weak in the knees; the foundation of secrets he had built his life on was swiftly crumbling to the ground.

* * *

FOURTEEN

The light blue Ford pickup charged into the drive throwing gravel everywhere. "Belle, Belle!" Sanford didn't even bother to close the door of his truck as he rushed inside the house and let the screen slam with more force than usual behind him.

"What is it, Sanford?" Belle stepped from the laundry room.

He tried to catch his breath. "We cannot have that woman over here for dinner!"

"What? Who are you talking about, San?" Belle drew him a glass of water from the kitchen sink. "Here now, drink this and tell me what's going on."

He led her by the hand to the sofa and pulled up a chair from the kitchen table to sit facing her.

"Belle, listen. Joe's ma is..." Sanford hesitated just long enough to alarm her.

"Joe's ma is *what?* Just say what's on your mind." She was becoming exasperated with him.

"Joe's ma is, Gracie." Sanford heard his words but still couldn't believe them.

"Gracie? *Your* Gracie? Well, Sanford, that's crazy talk. In case you haven't noticed, Eva's Joe is a white-skinned boy." Belle looked at Sanford as if she pitied him for being so ignorant.

"Joe is an *adopted* white boy. Apparently Gracie adopted him when he was just a youngin." Sanford added.

Belle stared at him for a moment. "Adopted? Well isn't that something. She traded her baby girl in for a son. Sounds like something she'd do. Well, we knew this day would come and now here it is staring us right in the face. We have to tell her, Sanford, like we should have done long ago."

Just then, Sissy and Eva rushed through the front door, returning home from vacation Bible school. "Mama," Eva hollered.

"We're right here, darling," Belle responded calmly.

"Oh, Daddy, you're here too. Good, I need to talk to you both about something important and I just can't wait another minute," Eva exclaimed.

Belle noticed the small cuts and scratches all over Eva's arms and legs. "What happened to you, girl?"

Eva was excited to tell her mother about the locket, when she noticed the outline of Belle's, lying beneath her collar where it always was. "I uh, just got into some weeds coming, home is, all."

"Sit down, Eva." Sanford's voice cracked.

"Sissy honey, why don't you change your clothes and go on down to the lake to cool off a bit? You can grab a biscuit on your way out to tide you over until dinnertime, looks like it's going to be a little late today."

"Why do I always have to be the one *leaving* the room? Can't I stay in here? I promise not to bother anybody. Please, please, please?" Sissy begged.

"Now you do as your mama told you to do and quit making trouble, young lady." Sanford rebuked his youngest.

Sissy screeched as she ran down the hallway to her bedroom but did exactly as she was told.

"Your father and I need to speak with you too, Eva, but why don't you start, sugar. What is it?" Belle asked.

"I was over at Miss Billy and Zoey's the other day, as you know, and well, they gave me an album with some old pictures of you and Daddy and all your friends when you were younger. Some things came up I want to know more about." Eva wondered if she was doing the right thing.

Belle sensed her daughter's apprehension. "It's all right, Eva. Feel free to ask us anything you need to."

Sanford sat quietly, regretting he had put this conversation off for so long.

Eva faced her father and tried to begin slowly, but the words blurted out against her will. "OK, then who is Gracie?"

It was Sanford's turn to be flabbergasted and he stuttered, not knowing what to say. "Well uh, slow down a minute now."

Sissy walked past the living room with a dry pastry in her hand, wearing her bright pink swimsuit, completely recovered from her nervous breakdown. "Holler when it's time to eat, Mama."

"All right, darling, you'll be the first to know." Belle grinned when Sissy leaned down for a kiss on the cheek before scurrying out the front door. Sanford was still unable to speak when Belle spoke up for him. "Gracie was your father's girlfriend before we were married, Eva." Sanford looked a little flustered that his wife was acting so casually toward the subject but Belle just shrugged her shoulders at him. "It's long overdue, Sanford."

He nodded his head and sighed. "You're right, Belle."

Eva relaxed a little when she saw her parents were more than willing to talk about it. "The way I hear it, they were in love. What I can't understand is, Daddy, why did you end up marrying Mama if you were in love with another girl?"

Sanford looked for Belle to save him again but she only smiled, knowing this was a question he needed to answer on his own.

He realized it too and began prudently. "Honey, it's true. I did love Gracie very much. You see, something happened that made her parents very upset, so they moved away before we even finished school. I never saw her again, plain and simple."

"That's it? What happened? Why would they do such a thing?" Eva needed to know.

Sanford moved from the chair to the sofa and took his daughter's hand, pulling her gently to sit between him and Belle. "Sometimes when you love someone, you make choices, uh, Gracie was pregnant, sweetheart. I didn't know it until much later." Sanford searched Eva's face for some response to the bomb he had dropped.

Eva was contemplative, trying to piece it all together in her young mind. "They were ashamed. You're saying they moved away because they were ashamed of their own daughter, huh?"

"Well yes, I suppose that's true. This is a small town, always has been, and with the Buhler's in charge of the church, well, they advised Gracie's parents to leave just as soon as they could."

Belle shuddered when she considered the amount of power and influence the Buhler's had always had over the community and her own life as well.

"When did you stop loving Gracie and start loving Mama?" Eva asked. Belle and Sanford were always surprised at their oldest daughter's ability to speak with more wisdom than a girl her age should have. Neither of them knew how to answer the question, because they had always understood their marriage was one built on friendship, not infatuation or passionate love. "I'm sorry, Mama. Is it bad of me to be talking about Daddy's old girlfriend?"

"Oh no, baby, I'm just thinking back to the day when your father proposed." Belle realized just how much the two of them had been through together and how their trust in one another ran deeper than many in a more conventional union.

The screen door slammed and Sissy stood before them covered head to toe in mud, holding a compliant terrapin.

"Aw shoot! Can't you go play a little while longer, Sissy child?" Eva exclaimed, not wanting to be interrupted.

"No! I'm getting hungry and I need a bath!" Sissy wailed, as she was at an age where her moods fluxed between mature and manic.

Belle rubbed her forehead, trying to remain patient. "Sissy, you and your turtle are going to have to go down to the lake and play until I call for you and I won't take any arguing from you neither."

Sanford gave Sissy a warning look and, astonished that Belle had scolded her so, Sissy's jaw hit the floor. She stomped out the front door, howling like a teething baby all the way down to the edge of the lake. The tension in the room seemed to lighten, as they laughed together at Sissy's childish behavior.

"Anyhow, where were we? Oh yes, your daddy asked me to marry him four years after we graduated from high school and I said yes." Belle finished explaining.

"So what ever happened to the baby? Gracie's baby, I mean?" Eva asked, throwing them off guard.

After so many years of trying to convince everyone they were living a normal life, a legitimate life, they had neglected to reveal the truth to the one who deserved to hear it most. How could they tell her that Gracie's baby recently turned fourteen years old and her name was Eva Dawn?

* * *

FIFTEEN

Julie London was crooning "Black Coffee" as Gracie swayed to the music wearing an emerald green negligee with a matching floor-length coverlet and full makeup, as if she were expecting someone that wasn't her son. Joe had never gotten entirely comfortable with his mother's sexy wardrobe she wore no matter what time of day it was. She had grown older just like the rest of her classmates but was still movie-star gorgeous as she exhaled gray smoke from the menthol-flavored cigarette she pinched between two nicotine-stained fingers. "How was work today, son?" she asked when Joe came through the door.

He rubbed his neck and set his lunch box on the kitchen table. He was hungry, but too tired to make himself something to eat. "I'm beat, tell you what." He fell into the sofa, still trying to get used to the aches and pains from his new job. "I had lunch with Mr. Johnson today, Ma. He seems like a real good man."

"Mr. Johnson? How do you know Mr. Johnson, son?" she asked, trying to sound indifferent.

"He's Eva's daddy, Ma." Joe was exasperated at his mother's inability to remember anything that didn't have to do with her.

Gracie sucked on her cigarette, blinking her Betty Boop eyelashes. "*Who* is Eva?" She pretended not to know.

Joe hung his head frustrated and, too exhausted to deal with her blatant self-centeredness. "You know, the girl I met in the woods? We were invited to their house for supper, week after next?"

"When you told me about the girl, you never once mentioned who her daddy was." She flapped her hands in the air like a bird, to dry her freshly painted cranberry, fingernails.

"Why? You know him?" Joe tested her.

"So what if I do?" Gracie feigned disinterest as she waddled on her heels toward the sofa with fluffy white cotton balls stuffed between her newly pedicured toes.

"Nothing if you do. It's just that we were talking today and he thinks maybe you two knew each other when you were kids is all," Joe explained, growing more curious about their relationship.

Gracie extended her hands out in front of her and puckered her Ruby Red Dress lips to blow hot air onto her wet nails.

"Really, what did he have to say about me?" Gracie sounded as if she were still in grade school.

"Nothing much, he just got a little nervous when I mentioned your name is all." He hoped to sound nonchalant as he recalled Sanford's odd behavior.

Gracie clutched the coffee table with her toes and painted over a smudge on the little piggy that went to market while she bit her burning cigarette between her teeth. "He got nervous, huh?"

"Well, maybe it was nothing." Joe wondered if he was making too much out of it.

"Hmm, maybe," Gracie snuffed out her cigarette and entertained the idea that Sanford might still care for her, ignoring the warning signals blaring from her conscience. "You know what, son? Suddenly I can't wait to meet your little girlfriend. It'd be nice to see Sanford and Belle again too. After all, we were all good friends at one time."

When he didn't respond, she was relieved to find he had fallen asleep. She needed some time to think about her scheme that was coming together so perfectly as far as she was concerned. A grin befitting a court jester stretched across her pretty painted face and she reclined on the sofa, lighting another smoke.

"Sanford *is* the reason I came back to this little nothing of a town." Gracie mumbled to herself. *So what if I, did hear about him marrying that tomboy Belle a long time ago. He obviously still feels something for me. Besides, it's only natural our baby girl should have her real parents together again.*

* * *

SIXTEEN

Belle stood at the screen door to check on Sissy who was playing contentedly under the maple trees. She seemed to be talking to herself as she plopped large blobs of mud onto the picnic table that would soon become little brown huts in her doll-sized village. Tiny shrubs were made from limbs she had snapped from the nearby bushes only a few feet away from the hidden stranger who was talking to her, making her his friend.

When Belle was satisfied that Sissy was safe, she returned to the sofa. "Well, Sanford?"

Sanford ran his hands nervously through his hair. "I guess we better back up a bit so it will all make sense to her, huh, Belle? Why don't you start?"

Belle gave him a look that called him a coward. "Well, let's see. I stayed living in this house after my parents died and just after graduation my very best friend moved away. I was so sad about it I just became a hermit, I guess you could say. Other than going to church on Sundays, I didn't see anybody. That's when I lost touch with Billy, Zoey, everybody I cared about to tell the truth. Without Ronny, I just didn't care about anything anymore until the day I got a phone call from your father."

"Why did you wait so long to call Mama, Daddy?" Eva asked. "I thought you all were friends."

"We were, but like your mama said, she just didn't want anyone around. Then I got some good news I hoped would cheer her up, help her move on from her sadness and I made her an offer I hoped she wouldn't refuse." Sanford took Belle's hand in his.

"What kind of offer?" Eva probed further.

Sanford cleared his throat. "Well, I heard from Gracie's mother Janey, calling to say Gracie had a little baby girl four years earlier and that I was the child's father."

Eva couldn't believe her ears. "You're the one who got Gracie pregnant? Why didn't she tell you herself?"

"I don't think her parents gave her much of a chance. I was thrilled to know I was a daddy, I just wished I'd known sooner. Anyhow, Janey felt I should take the baby on account of Gracie being too busy to care for it on her own." Sanford waited for his words to sink in.

Eva was looking through the eyes of a child, revolted at the very idea. "Too busy, who could be too busy to take care of their own baby?"

"You see, Gracie was so young and she liked going out with her friends like all youngsters do. Her parents felt a baby was just too much for them to handle at their age, so they couldn't keep her neither," Belle added, trying to help her understand.

"Gracie's father was against telling me about the baby so he didn't even know Janey had called me that night," Sanford recalled, as if it were only yesterday. "Anyhow, she said we could meet the next evening at Junior's Piggly Wiggly, on one condition. I could never contact Gracie and tell her I was the one taking the child. All she knew was that Janey, was going to find a home for her, but she never knew where or who with."

"How could Gracie be so cruel? I mean, the girl was four years old. How could she just give her up like that?" Eva exclaimed.

"Sometimes we're forced to make decisions we don't want to make and that's just the way life is. It's no good to put blame or judgment on folks, because we don't know what we might do if we were ever in the same situation," Belle enlightened her.

"That's right, darling, which brings us to answering your question about me calling your mama after all those years. I asked her to marry me and help me raise the child. I knew she needed something more in her life than what she was living and I needed someone I could trust and count on to help me be a good father." Sanford hoped this wasn't too overwhelming for her to accept all at once.

Eva stared at her feet, reviewing the story of the disregarded child. "There's still one question you haven't answered, Daddy." She began slowly; hesitantly as if suddenly unsure whether or not she was truly ready for the answers she was seeking.

Sanford held his breath.

"Where is she now? After you and Mama were married, what happened to the girl?" Memories of the beautiful woman in the photograph flashed through her mind and she suddenly remembered why she looked so familiar. Eva cried out loud as the veil slowly lifted, allowing the long-awaited truth to be revealed.

* * *

SEVENTEEN

"You don't plan on being home any earlier than five thirty, do you, son?" Gracie sipped her coffee and smoked a cigarette as she sat with Joe at the kitchen table.

"Why, Ma?" he asked, heaping one last spoonful of mashed potatoes and gravy onto his baking powder biscuit. Gracie had just rolled out of bed even though it was well past noon. She wore bobby pins in her hair and a pink velour robe trimmed in satin.

"It's just a question. Can't a mother wonder what her son is doing at the end of the day?" Gracie glanced up from her coffee cup with her usual pose of child-like naiveté. He raised one eyebrow, recognizing the all-too familiar behavior of his naughty mother.

"You're up to no good, Ma. I can see it in the way you're acting. Good thing I decided to come home for lunch today. There's no telling what kind of trouble you'd be stirring up if I hadn't," he teased her, but really meant what he said.

"Oh, Joe, you talk like an old lady. I'm not up to anything. Now, you get on out of here before you're late getting back to work," Gracie chided, leading him to the front door before handing him his leather work gloves.

"Ma, please. I know you're a grown woman but whatever you're up to, be good and be careful," he advised her as if she were an adolescent.

"Well, I can't do both now, can I, boy? HA!" She slapped him on the back playfully and pushed him firmly out the door when the wooden bird coo-cooed one o'clock.

"All right, all right, I'm going." Joe leaned down to kiss his petite mother on the forehead then walked the path toward the mill. How he wished she would grow up and act her age.

"You're a big boy, son. This is no big deal, all right now?" she hollered at his back, but he didn't turn to answer her.

Gracie closed the door and kneeled on the couch, to watch Joe through the window until he was out of sight then hurried to the stereo to slide Peggy Lee onto the turntable. She loved how her skin tingled when the beauty sang, "Fever." She went to her bedroom and dropped her robe to the floor, revealing a black lace negligee and sheer black thigh-high stockings. *One final touch,* she slipped into her shiny black, baby doll heels, viewing her reflection in the vanity mirror. *What am I doing? He's a married man, but he belonged to me long before he married her.* She choked, blinking back the tears that filled her bottom lids.

A halo formed around her pixie face as she pulled one last bobby pin from her short, brown hair. After spraying Tabu on her inner thighs, she finished with one soft shot to her cleavage, ignoring the tedious details haunting her afflicted mind of a baby girl born and forsaken but not forgotten.

Things are different now and I want what I was forced to leave behind. She freshened up her Pink Champagne lipstick one last time as her long, slender cigarette smoldered in the aluminum tray with the sand pillow bottom. The smoke stung her eyes, clouding her vision until the knock at the door promised all of her dreams were about to come true.

* * *

EIGHTEEN

Eve Boswell sang loud and clear, from the stereo speakers Belle had set out on the front porch. The tune, "Heat Wave," seduced her as she dived off the wooden dock into the lake, leaving just a hint of a splash at the end of her toes. The water was unusually cool and clear in that part of Missouri and it trickled from her ebony locks when she popped up through the center of the black inner tube. Her naked, cinnamon brown body hung in the frigid water, reminding her she was still alive as she twirled one sun streaked curl around her pinky finger, grateful for the time alone to think.

Who would believe this was the same Belle who attended church faithfully and required her family to pray before every meal? So relaxed so beautiful so *real*, she was when Sanford and the girls left her alone and went to town every week.

As she gazed at the changing colors of the maple leaves, her thoughts drifted back to the days when she was a young girl, playing with Ronny Jean and feeling happy, *truly* happy. She dropped down under the tube and swam to shore to sit at the picnic table and to fill her glass from the half full pitcher of hard lemonade. Belle had found the red photo album under Eva's pillow that morning when she was changing the sheets on her bed and she was savoring every single photograph as it laid open on the table.

An enchanting girl wearing a white swimsuit smiled up at her from one of her favorite photographs of Ronny. She turned it over and kissed it tenderly as she read the familiar writing, "Blue Belle and Ronny Jean, best friends 4 ever." Her body trembled slightly when she returned it to the clear plastic pocket she had taken it from.

Belle guzzled her drink, attempting to ease the constant tightness in her chest. She filled her glass again and waded back out into the water and sat in the inner tube. When she rested her glass in her cleavage, the cold prickled her skin, arousing something primitive within her. As she stared out over the lake she was consumed with questions that always haunted her. *Where are you, Ron? What happened that day you left? Will we ever be together again?*

"Find your way home to me, Ronny. Find your way back home." A gentle breeze whispered through the trees and across her sun-kissed skin, making her shiver. She wrapped her arms protectively around her exposed body when she thought she saw someone moving in the trees. Grinning at her own silliness, she decided it was only her imagination due to the amount of liquid lightning she had consumed. A cloud passed over the sun, reminding her it was almost time for her family to come home. Feeling comfortably numb, she slid from the tube and waded to shore, wrapping herself in a terry cloth robe the color of cornflowers.

With the photographs tucked under her arm, she carried the glass and empty pitcher up the hill and into the house. The record album turned silently under the needle and Belle paused for a moment to enjoy the quiet, to feel what her home was like when there was no chaos, no people to tend to, only her thoughts and memories to occupy the space around her.

She set the glassware on the kitchen counter before rushing to her bedroom where she removed her dingy, graying calico print dress from the bent wire hanger, wondering when the charade would end.

"This is getting old," she admitted wearily, sliding the worn-out dress up over her hips. She took the silver locket from her dresser and opened it for one last look at her Ronny, kissing the tiny photograph before snapping it shut and fastening the clasp at the back of her neck. Feeling the warmth of the metal beneath the thin layer of cloth gave her comfort as she finished securing the last tiny button at her throat.

Belle checked her costume in the mirror and held her head up high, resuming character as all actresses do before going on stage, hoping to convince their audience. She skimmed her fingers through her soft black curls, attempting a deep breath that always stopped at shallow, when the screen door slammed, right on cue.

"Hey, Mama," Sissy squealed.

Fully aware she had ingested at least one too many beverages, Belle's head swam as she came to greet her family, pretending to be ready for them expecting dinner on the table. "Hi, girls, how was your day? You all are so late I was starting to worry a bit."

"Oh, we're just fine, Mama. Daddy dropped us off at the movie house to see a matinee and was a little late picking us up is all," Sissy explained, setting a bag of groceries on the counter.

Belle knew this was not at all like Sanford. "Dropped you off? I thought you were going to see a movie together and pick up some groceries after. Where is your father, anyway?"

"He's in the truck, still. I'll go get him," Sissy offered, running out the door.

Eva remained quiet. She hadn't spoken a single word to Sanford or Belle since learning the truth about her birth mother. She had nearly fainted that day when she remembered Gracie as her absent mother and thought of her grandparents who didn't want her. Belle and Sanford had been desperate to make her smile, as they missed their oldest daughter with the usual quick wit and unbridled enthusiasm.

The awkward silence was unnerving, so Belle attempted to make conversation with Eva as if everything would be just fine.

"I'm running a tad bit behind myself. Just one of those days, I suppose." She tied an apron around her waist before taking a bumpy-skinned chicken from the refrigerator and laying it on the cutting board. The pig lard she scooped from the metal can, melted instantly in the cast-iron skillet when she turned the white knob that caused the flame to rise.

Belle was concerned when Sissy came back into the house alone with another bag of groceries. "Honey, *where* is your father?"

"He says he needs a minute or two. He was awful quiet all the way home, like he's sick or something." Sissy shrugged her shoulders as Sanford entered the house. His face was ashen, mirroring death itself as he closed the screen door softly, slowly behind him.

"Well, that's a first in this house," Belle commented casually, giving the chicken a whack with the cleaver. She dipped a bloody thigh into a mixture of raw eggs and milk then rolled it in a pie plate filled with seasoned flour and cornmeal. When Sanford didn't reply, she turned to face him. "Sanford, what's the matter? You don't look so good. Are you ill?" Sanford's downcast face told Belle that something was terribly wrong.

"Girls, I want you to go and feed the cows and chickens before you come and eat. Give them some fresh water too, now," Belle instructed them.

Sissy started for the door but Eva sat still. "OK Mama. We'll be back in just a bit. Come on, Eva!" Sissy ordered her older sister.

Eva stood begrudgingly, stomping across the kitchen floor to follow Sissy outside. Once the girls were gone, Belle inspected her husband, who was wringing his hat in his hands, unable to look his wife in the eye.

Belle turned back to preparing dinner, peeling the potatoes over the sink, waiting for Sanford to speak. "Well, Sanford, I assume you need to talk, so go on."

Sanford felt sick to his stomach as the familiar sounds and smells of home made him wonder why he had done what he had done.

"I went to see her, Belle. I told myself I just wanted to cancel the dinner plans and I called her on the telephone. Next thing I knew, she invited me for coffee and I went to see her!" The words spilled from his mouth and his bowels relaxed as he revealed the details of his circumstantial indiscretion.

Belle froze, not turning to face him. She swallowed hard, allowing the meaning of his words to wash over her like water over a pitcher of ice, as she slid a heavily coated chicken leg easily into the pan of melted suet. The grease popped and crackled as it drowned the raw meat, momentarily hypnotizing her as she realized this routine once represented her duties as a wife and mother, but suddenly held no significance whatsoever.

"I guess what you're saying is, you two did more than just drink coffee and talk?" She didn't know how else to proceed with the unexpected dialogue, adding a breast to the skillet.

"Yes, Belle, we didn't mean for it to happen, I swear! I just wanted to tell her you and I, are the ones who raised Eva and that she is doing just fine!" Sanford was emotional.

Belle closed her eyes and her mouth began to water as if she were going to throw up. "Maybe she doesn't, want her to know. Did you even stop to think of Eva's feelings about it?"

"My feelings about what," Eva startled them both. She hadn't uttered a word in so long they didn't know whether to be happy or upset that she was eavesdropping on their private conversation from the porch.

"Eva! How long have you been standing there, child? You're supposed to be doing your chores!" Sanford scolded her more harshly than he intended to.

"We did them, Daddy, and now we're through," Eva replied through the screen, with Sissy standing behind her. "What else haven't you told me?"

Belle shuddered visibly and grabbed the edge of the counter to keep her balance. She turned slowly to face her husband with an expression that pierced him through the heart, staring deep into his eyes as if seeing him for the first time in her life.

Sanford awaited his punishment, expecting her to yell, scream, and holler at him for being unfaithful after all they had been through together.

Beyond marriage, beyond children, beyond the façade, the one consistent element in their arrangement was trust. Black smoke rose up from the forgotten meat that needed turning, as Belle slid to the floor, laughing hysterically, finally able to breathe.

* * *

NINETEEN

As Billy and Zoey drove into town to do their monthly errands, they admired the leaves on the trees that were turning many shades of vibrant reds and yellows.

They went to the post office first, wanting to see their friend who had recently lost his wife to cancer. "Howdy, Earl didn't see your car outside. You take up walking to work?" Billy greeted their longtime buddy who stood behind the mail counter wearing his uniform of blue. He was a dark-colored man in his late fifties with a skiff of gray hair striping each temple and a smile that brightened every room he entered.

"Well, hey there Miss Billy, Zoey. Yeah, I've got no choice for the time being since my car, caught on fire the other night, just busted into flames. Isn't that the strangest thing?" Earl chuckled as if the incident were no big deal.

Billy wrinkled her nose at the news. "The hell you say, Earl? How on earth does a car just catch fire like that?"

"Well, I'm ashamed to say it, but I might have left a ciggy burning in the tray. I tried taking up smoking again after Bonnie died thinking it would help calm my nerves but that did it for me there. I'm never going to smoke again," Earl vowed.

It all sounded fishy to Billy and it bothered her that he was so easygoing about it. "That doesn't sound right, Earl. It just doesn't make any sense."

"Homer thinks he can fix it good as new. Well *almost* new. All I lost was the front seat, so I'll be driving again in no time. Now, ladies, what can I do for you anyhow? You come to get your mail, or do you just miss me?" Earl teased.

"Nope, just needing our mail is all." Billy returned the friendly banter.

Zoey blushed at her partner's never-ending ability to enter a room with more brass and sass than anyone should, as far as she was concerned. It was also a part of Billy she found to be incredibly endearing.

Earl chuckled at the witty comebacks he could always count on from his friend. "Here you go, Bill. How you two doing out there in the boonies? Still got that fine garden?" Earl handed Billy a stack of white and manila envelopes.

"Oh yeah, always will have. It's what we do, you know? Speaking of, we brought you some zucchini and tomatoes," Billy announced proudly.

"Oh, I almost forgot. I'll fetch them from the truck, Bill." Zoey said, rushing out the door.

"How are you holding up Earl, you're looking good, but I know it's been a hard road for you without your Bonnie," Billy was sympathetic.

Earl considered Billy to be a true friend and the only person he would indulge with his true feelings. "Oh, I'm doing all right, Bill. Night time is the hardest for me."

"Well, Earl, you and Bonnie did everything together. You're bound to feel the loneliness. I know it's not even Halloween yet, but why don't you plan on coming out to our place next month for Thanksgiving dinner? We'd love to have you," Billy offered sincerely.

"Careful now Bill, I might just take you up on that and the way your Zoey cooks, you might not get rid of me." Earl grinned.

Zoey returned with a brown paper bag full of zucchini and Brandywine tomatoes and a pie plate covered with a red and white striped linen towel.

"Here you go now, Earl." Zoey set the bag on the counter and lifted one corner of the towel to reveal a freshly baked apple pie. "We brought you a little treat too."

Earl brightened at the gesture and closed his eyes as he leaned in closer to catch a whiff of the aromatic cinnamon and cloves. "MM-*mm*, you do make the very best pies in all of Missouri, Zoey. Thank you ladies, you're always so good to me."

"We're just ensuring you won't go snooping through our mail." Billy continued to gibe playfully.

"Too late, too late, I already snooped," Earl retorted jovially.

"Well, it's been fun as always, Earl, but we best get going now. Zoey here needs to get some quilting supplies from Polly's. We'll be seeing you next month though," Billy promised, waving the envelopes in the air.

"Bye, Earl." Zoey waved with a smile as Billy opened the door allowing her out ahead of her. "Billy, you're a terrible woman, teasing Earl so."

"Oh, if I didn't harass him so bad, he'd think I was mad at him." Billy felt lucky to have such a friend as Earl.

In the spirit of fall, orange and white twinkle lights framed the storefront window of Polly's Patchworks and a bell jingled above the door, announcing their arrival. A bleached, platinum blonde haired woman with a low-cut blouse and a high-cut skirt, poked her head out from the back room, holding an unusually large coffee mug in one hand and a lit cigarette in the other.

"Well hey, Zoey, Miss Billy. Always good to see you girls! Has it been a month already?" She set the cup down on her desk and tossed the lipstick stained filter onto the floor before crushing it under the toe of her pump.

"What say, Polly girl, you're looking lovely as ever," Zoey replied, as Polly trotted toward them with her plentiful breasts bouncing and jiggling, threatening to leap out of her brassiere with every click of her high heels.

Billy took a seat on the bench in the front of the store. "How goes it Pol? I'll be over here looking through the mail while you do what you need to do, OK, Zoe?"

Polly gave Zoey a big hug before trying to persuade her to buy some beautifully hand-dyed satin material she had received only the day before. "Look at this exquisite fabric here, Zoe. I can see you wearing it as a fancy dress."

Fully aware that Polly was the most influential salesperson in town, Zoey eyed her keenly. "Girl, what do I need with a dress? You should be down at Smithy's selling cars!"

"All right, all right, can't blame a girl for trying. What *do* you need, then?" Polly smiled and winked at Zoey. She was having fun with her as always.

Billy enjoyed the familiar dance between the two old friends that was always the same. Polly would try to entice Zoey into buying the newest, most expensive fabrics and Zoey would always refuse her, only to end up spending twice as much money than she would have, had she purchased what Polly suggested in the first place. Of course Zoey was a frugal shopper and always left the store with twice as many items as well.

Billy continued sorting the usual bills and advertisements into two separate piles when she noticed a letter with a return address she didn't recognize. Her brow furrowed as she slid the file of her fingernail clippers under the flap and removed the folded paper from inside. As she read the words written in a vaguely familiar hand, the goose bumps started to rise.

Dear Billy,

I hope you still have this address or that your parents will see to it you receive this letter, as I don't know where else to start. Everything that's happened since the day I left town has been a nightmare. My father hid me in the woods so he could do what you know he has always done to me and I don't know how to say this but just plain and simple. I stabbed him and set him on fire before I ran away and I thought I killed him. I turned myself in to the police and when they went to find the shack where I left him there was no sign of his body. They found his car with blood on the seat too, so they think he's gone back to Stockton. The only good thing about it is, if I end up going to jail, it won't be for murder. I think it would have been worth it, just to know he was gone from this earth once and for all. I know Blue must have been so scared for me the day I left. Please tell her I'm fine now, as I live with a nice couple. They are both retired professors from the college here in Hannibal, and they take good care of me and are helping me get back on my feet. I want to come home but the police say this is the safest place I can be for now since Manson's probably trying to hunt me down back home.

Is Blue well? Does she miss me too? I just couldn't let her see me the way I was when the Montgomery's found me. I was just a hollow shell and I know it would have killed her to see me that way. I still have a long way to go and I admit I'm a little worried that Blue may have found someone new to love after all these years. I miss you all so much. Please write back just as soon as you can.

Love to all,
Ronny Jean

Billy thrust the page into the air. "Oh dear God, it's Ronny, it's our Ronny Jean, Zoe!" She hopped up and down excitedly.

Zoey peered from behind a bolt of cloth she and Polly were holding in the air, inspecting the pattern. "What's that you say, Bill?"

"Our Ronny has written us a letter!" Billy repeated, impatiently.

Polly stumbled, struggling to keep the material from touching the floor, when Zoey dropped her end of the bolt and dashed to the front of the store. She quickly scanned the note that begged for any hope that Belle still loved Ronny.

"We're going to have to tell her, aren't we, Bill?" Zoey asked.

Polly pretended not to listen as she waited patiently at the cutting table for Zoey to tell her how many yards she should cut from each fabric she had chosen.

"Think about it. Belle is married to Sanford and then there's, the girls to consider as well. No sir-ee, too many lives are involved, too many people who could be hurt," Billy decided.

"I didn't think about all of that, Bill, and I know you're right. On the other hand, Belle needs to know!" Zoey disagreed.

"OK now, let's think about it a bit. The least we can do is get on home and write Ron a letter. We'll let her decide what she wants us to do. You finish up with Polly there, while I go get the Scout," she said.

On her way back to the quilting shop Billy noticed Eunice Buhler coming out of her mother's house. The stiff, saintly woman looked nervous and suspicious as she closed and locked the front door then stepped hurriedly down the sidewalk toward Billy keeping her head down so she wouldn't have to make eye contact.

"Howdy, Buhler, you're looking mighty fine today." Billy hoped to rile her up just a bit.

Buhler scowled at her. "Why don't you homos mind your own business and stay hidden in the woods where you belong?" she grumbled, not stopping to chat.

"But then you'd never get to see me," Billy replied with unconcealed sarcasm. She couldn't believe the closed-minded ignorance some people still displayed and shook her head as she went back inside the quilting shop.

"Let me get those for you Zoe." Billy took the bags from her so she could pay Polly.

"Oh, thank you, Billy girl. What do I owe you Polly?" Zoey asked, pulling her wallet from her pack.

"Was that young Buhler I saw huffing past you just now, Bill?" Polly asked handing Zoey her receipt.

"Sure enough was, Pol. Whoo-ee! God made some folks harder to love than others," she concluded with dismay.

"Oh, isn't that the truth about it? Of course, some folks think she's been getting some loving from Manson here lately," Polly gossiped the way she liked to do.

"What's that you say, Polly?" Zoey asked eagerly.

Billy leaned in closer, not wanting to miss a single word. "The hell you say, Pol. We're all ears."

"Well, some folks say they've seen Manson sneaking around inside the Buhler house when they're walking by." Polly blathered. "I've seen him myself matter of fact."

"Are you absolutely sure it's Manson Pol?" Billy wanted some facts to balance out the drama.

"Oh, am I ever. I was just coming to work one day minding my own business when there he was, larger than life, pushing old Buhler in her wheelchair to the breakfast table." Polly recounted the events as Billy and Zoey glanced discreetly at one another. They knew full well Polly didn't know how to mind her own business because she just wasn't made that way.

"Did you tell the police?" Zoey asked.

Polly kept on, "Uh huh, I called them and told them what I saw on account of them being in here just last week asking about him."

"It would make sense that the foster son would come home to Mama when he needed help the most, wouldn't it? So what did the police say?" Billy was completely convinced it was Manson.

"Well, they said they'd had other folks saying the same thing, including the good Dr. Betty Phelps. Anyhow, I watched them with my own eyes knocking on the door and talking to Beatrice then they just turned and walked away, like no big deal," Polly added, shrugging her shoulders.

"Old Buhler still has the power, doesn't she? Well it's been a very interesting and informative visit. Keep us posted on any new developments, won't you Pol?" Billy guided Zoey toward the door.

Polly loved an invitation to tell what she knew. "You know I will girls, you know I will. I suppose you already heard our friend Gracie's back in town, huh?"

They stopped and the bell above the door tinkled unnoticed. "Excuse me, Pol? I thought I heard you say Gracie's back in town." Billy chuckled nervously.

Polly continued to inform her friends. "Oh yeah, she *and* her boy, you mean to tell me she hasn't even been out to see you yet? Guess they moved into the Henry place just down the street there. Everybody tries to leave but they always find their way back home, huh girls?"

* * *

TWENTY

"Mama, are you all right?" Eva squealed, rushing to Belle's side.

Belle was warmed by the sound of her daughter's concern for her. "Yes, yes, darling, I'm fine. I just need a drink of water, if you don't mind."

"Get a cool rag for her head, Sissy, and turn off the fire on the stove!" Sanford hollered and sat on the floor next to Belle before taking her hand into his. "Blue Belle, I'm so sorry." He brought their joined hands to his cheek and began to cry.

"Here, Mama." Sissy laid a cool, damp cloth on her mother's forehead and Eva handed her a glass of water.

"What's going on, Mama?" Eva felt plagued by the recent events that continued to surface.

Belle looked Eva in the eye. "Let me tell you something, girl of mine. There's a whole lot happening in a very short amount of time that you need to know, and no matter what comes, your father and I love you and Sissy more than anything in the world. We would never do anything to hurt either one of you." Eva looked away, feeling ashamed of her own behavior toward her parents. "Do you understand? I know you're angry with us for keeping secrets from you all these years but we did it, because we love you and thought it was best. If we were wrong about that, we're sorry, but we did what we felt we had to do to protect you. Now, if you're saying you're grown enough to know the truth, then you're going to have to prove it by accepting it as it comes."

Eva's eyes met Belle's once again. "OK, Mama. I know what you're saying and I'm sorry for pouting for so long." They hugged and Eva laid her head on Belle's chest. "You've always been my mama and you always will be."

"All right, my child, that is what I need to know, because you will always be my oldest baby no matter how long you decide to pout and go without speaking to me." Belle grinned, as she held Eva's face in her hands and wiped the tears from her cheeks with her thumbs. "Now listen, honey, there is much more we need to discuss if you think you want to know, but for right now, your Daddy and me need to have a private discussion and I'm going to ask you to call Miss Billy and Zoey and ask if you two can go have dinner with them tonight, all right?"

"But Mama," Sissy whined, feeling insecure at seeing her father cry and her mother lying on the floor.

"Sissy, hush! All right, Mama, I'll call them." Eva sounded more like herself, again.

Sanford helped Belle to her feet while Eva made the call to Billy and Zoey. "They want to know if we can spend the night, Mama."

"Tell them yes and thank you, that would be wonderful, darling. You girls go pack a bag and start on over there. Stay on the trail and don't forget to take a sweatshirt. It's starting to get cold at night. I'll call you in the morning." Belle leaned on Sanford for support as the blood rushed much too swiftly to her head, making her dizzy and nauseous. She made a silent vow to never again go without eating before drinking a pitcher of her special lemonade.

Eva and Sissy did as they were told and kissed their parents before walking out the door. "Miss Billy says they'll meet us halfway," Eva said.

"Love you," they sang in unison.

"We love you too, girls, more than you know," Sanford responded. They watched as the two made their way down the trail and Belle wasted no time.

"Sanford?" she began.

Sanford was distraught and white as a sheet even though Belle tried to calm him. "Belle I..." He began.

"Let's have a seat." She grabbed the pitcher of tea from the refrigerator on their way to the dining table and Sanford poured some into two glasses. Considering the dinner that was smoldering on the back of the stove, Belle filled a basket with biscuits and dipped one crudely into a jar of honey before biting into it. She chased it down with a gulp of cold tea. "Listen," she talked with a mouth full of food. "We both know your love for Gracie didn't die when she left and now here she is living in the same town again as you and me."

"Yes, but what we have..." Sanford started.

"What we *have* is something that is unfortunately built on lies but, more importantly, on our trust in one another. We gave each other a full life but the truth is the truth. You still love Gracie and I have never stopped loving Ronny and we both know it." Belle laid the facts down hard on the table.

"What are you saying?" Sanford searched her expression for clarity.

Belle tried to choose her words wisely. "I'm saying it's time to let it all go. I cry all the time because I can't live this way anymore and neither can you. Besides, we both know it's been over for quite some time."

"Seems so, huh? I know why you've been so unhappy. I just didn't know how to bring it up," Sanford admitted feebly. "So, now where do we go from here?"

"We both know we got into this marriage for Eva's sake and God knows she needed a mother that would love her. But you and I needed something from it too. You needed someone you could trust to help raise your daughter and I needed, well, I suppose I needed some way to try and convince folks I'm someone I'm really not." Belle's words drifted when she heard how ridiculous it all sounded now that she had lived a day or two past her teens.

"Belle, who you are, is a wonderful, loving woman with a heart of gold. The girls couldn't have asked for a better mother and God knows you've been the best wife a man could ever want." Sanford meant every word.

"Oh, I know that now, Sanford, but back then, I was younger and I did what I thought I had to do to keep the Buhler's off my back. You and I both know they're responsible for what happened to Ronny and without her, being true, to myself just didn't seem to matter anymore."

"I'm sorry I was unfaithful. I said I went to see Gracie to tell her about Eva but the truth is, once I knew she was back in town I just couldn't get her off my mind. When I showed up at her place, she was wearing next to nothing…" Sanford stopped talking when he realized Belle could do without the tawdry details.

Belle eyed him and chuckled at the irony of the situation. "Sanford, if I was to ever have the great fortune of hearing my Ronny was back in town, I would do the same thing. Believe you me, I wouldn't even hesitate. I don't want you hanging yourself for this, but now we need a plan because we've got two daughters counting on us to take care of them and they don't need to be hurt in any unnecessary ways while we're trying to figure out what we're going to do. Agreed?"

Sanford hugged his wife and best friend and kissed her gently on the cheek, "Agreed."

"One more thing, Sanford," she added.

"What is it?" Sanford wondered what more there could be.

"What did Gracie say when you told her about Eva?"

"She was so shocked I thought I was going to have to call a doctor to get her to settle down." Sanford sounded sympathetic to Gracie's position in the situation.

"Uh huh, sure she was," she said sarcastically.

A heavy-handed knock came unexpectedly at the front door and Sanford jumped out of his chair with Belle following close behind him. They were surprised to find Joe standing on the other side of the screen.

"Well, Joe. What are you doing here, son?" Sanford asked.

"Evening, sir, ma'am, I'm sorry to show up unannounced, but I was hoping to speak with Eva if I could." He sounded troubled.

Sanford opened the door respectfully. "She's not here. She and Sissy went on around the lake to Miss Billy's place. I don't expect you've met her yet but she and her partner Zoey are real good friends of ours. Eva's going to be real disappointed she missed you."

Joe was visibly agitated. "Are you sure about that, Mr. Sanford, because, my ma just told me we're not coming for supper on Sunday after all and I was wondering why Eva changed her mind about seeing me."

"Whoa, hold on now, Joe; don't go jumping to any conclusions. Eva had nothing to do with it, I can promise you that." Sanford didn't know how to continue under the circumstances.

"We all uh, your mother, Sanford, and me, decided we wanted to wait a bit on the supper plans is all. Eva still wants to see you, don't worry about that," Belle reassured him.

The obvious worry on his face softened. "Do you mean it? I was just really looking forward to my ma meeting Eva, is, all."

"Don't fret about it, she'll get the chance." Sanford glanced at Belle. "Anyway, it's starting to get dark out otherwise I'd suggest you go see her. Why don't we have her give you a call when she gets home first thing tomorrow morning?" Sanford suggested.

Joe smiled from ear to ear at the thought of Eva calling him on the telephone. "Yes sir, I surely would appreciate it."

He shook Sanford's hand and left, glad he had decided to show up at the Johnson house. Even though Eva wasn't there, he still got what he had come for. Confirmation she still wanted to see him.

They said their good-byes and Sanford and Belle sat back down at the table. "Well, where were we?" Sanford felt like his head was full of cobwebs after a day of so much emotion.

"You were just telling me how Gracie reacted to finding out that Eva has been living here with you and me all these years. Now we need to decide how we're going to tell Eva that Joe's mama is uh, *her* mama." Belle was frustrated with Sanford for not taking Eva's feelings into consideration before talking to Gracie.

"I think we just need to tell her straight out. We got this ball rolling and there's no stopping it now," Sanford reasoned.

Belle thought about it for a moment. "Then what, Sanford, after we tell her, what happens with you and me from there? You know I'm going to do my best to find Ronny."

Sanford scratched his head. "I don't know. I suppose for the girls' sake, we live here in this house together as long as we can make it work. They still deserve to grow up with a mother and father. That hasn't changed any."

"But are they really better off if we're still living a lie? I guess the rest we just work out one day at a time as it comes to us and lately it *is* coming to us," Belle acknowledged wearily.

"Belle," Sanford began seriously.

"Yes, Sanford, what is it?" Belle asked.

"I hope you find Ronny and I believe you will. I don't know how to thank you for all that you've done to help me all these years. Your life would have been so different if you hadn't agreed to marry me and take on my daughter. God knows my own life would have been a whole lot harder without you. Did I ever tell you so?" Sanford asked.

"There's no need to thank me, San. Eva's just as much my daughter as she is yours. Sissy's a bonus blessing and I wouldn't have missed this ride for anything in the world."

Without having to say so, they recognized the friendship they would always have with one another. Belle stood from her chair to get two tissues from the box on the counter and held one out to Sanford. "All right then, first things first," she announced through a sniffle.

"What's that, Belle?" Sanford wiped his tears and blew his nose.

Belle untied her apron and tossed it onto the table. "I am *dying* to get out of this dress!"

* * *

TWENTY-ONE

Dear Ronny Jean,
 Girl, we cannot believe we got a letter from you. We have been so worried and missing you like you can't believe. Zoe and I are still going strong after all these years. She moved in when my parents went to Texas to be closer to my brother and his wife. They felt the calling to be with their grandbabies, you know.

 Enough of all that. Listen, Ron, Belle is fine but me, and Zoe feel you should know what's been going on before we tell Belle we heard from you. That way you can decide what you want to do from there.

 Four years after you left, Belle and Sanford got hitched. It has nothing to do with love, you see, but Belle knew, like the *rest of us, that the Buhler's were partly responsible for you being treated the way you were by your folks. Marrying Sanford was her way of protecting herself from dangers of discrimination that sadly still linger with some who don't know any better. It has been a real protection for us to live out here in the woods like we do and there's only a very few we can be open with in town. The truth is Belle doesn't even come around here to see us. She makes sure her daughters do, though. I think it's her roundabout way of keeping in touch without putting herself in harm's way. I think seeing us only reminds her of you and the times we all had together too. It changed her whole life to lose you, Ron. She hasn't been the same since.*

We believe she'll come around when she's good and ready to do so and when she does, we'll be here with open arms.

Anyway, we know she still loves you, she just didn't know where to turn without you.

Do what you can to get back home, darling. We're still here and we promise not to say anything to Belle until you give us the go-ahead. She'll be so happy to know you're with good people that can help you and keep you safe.

We're so proud of you for finally standing up to Manson and fighting back! If you'd have killed him, we would have had a party! The police have been around here looking for him and we're almost positive he's hiding out at the Buhler house. Hope we can be the ones to turn the SOB in for you.

We love you!
Billy and Zoe

Billy read the letter out loud to Zoey as they hurried down the trail to meet the girls. "Sounds good," Zoey approved, when she was finished reading. Billy licked the envelope shut just as Eva and Sissy came into view.

"Remember now don't say a word about Ronny." Billy whispered.

"Well why would I, silly?" Zoey batted her eyes, trying to look innocent as they approached the girls and hugged them close. "Well, what a treat we get to see you again so soon, Eva darling, and look who you brought with you. Sissy child, well, aren't you just growing into a pretty little flower?"

Sissy grinned proudly, feeling the heat rise on the back of her neck at the compliment.

"Let's get home and carve some pumpkins, all righty girls?" Billy suggested. The four women moved quickly, trying to beat the setting sun and the older two kept an eye out for Manson.

Before they went into the house they walked through the pumpkin patch, each one choosing just the right pumpkin to carve for Halloween. When they went inside, they deposited their soon to be Jack-o-lanterns onto the kitchen counter then Eva followed Billy down the hallway and into the guest room with their bags.

"How are you doing, sugar, you look a little worn around the edges," Billy commented, when she noticed Eva's puffy eyes and solemn demeanor.

"I don't know. I guess I've been through a lot since I last saw you, Miss Billy," Eva responded wearily.

Billy wrapped her arm around the distraught girl and guided her gently to sit on the bed before taking a seat next to her. "Hang on a minute." Billy stepped out the door to peek into the kitchen where she saw Sissy sitting on the counter, pouring sugar from a measuring cup into a large stainless steel bowl. She talked on and on about her turtles and mud houses. Zoey caught Billy's eye and nodded to let her know she understood she and Eva needed some time to talk.

Billy returned to the bedroom, closing the door behind her. "What's happened, sweetheart? Why did your folks send you over here tonight, anyhow? We're so glad to have you, but you and I both know they've never done that before, don't we?"

"I know the truth," Eva said unexpectedly, sobbing.

"What truth is that, darling?" Billy asked softly.

"Mama isn't really my mama," she gushed.

Billy sat quietly for a moment with her arm around the reality-inflicted youth. "What do you mean your mama isn't your mama? She's the only one I've ever known you to have."

"The picture, the one of Gracie, she looked so familiar to me when we were going through the album, because she's my *real* mama. She gave me away when I was just four years old!" Eva continued to sob with the strong tone of resentment. "Did you know this whole time? Why didn't you tell me?" Eva was surprised at the displaced anger she felt toward Billy.

Billy's eyes widened, as it hadn't occurred to her that Eva would assume she knew anything about it. "Now, Eva, you have to remember, we didn't see or hear anything from your mama Belle until well, until we ran into each other at the market when you were nearly six years old. You remember that day?"

Eva tried to think, tugging a tissue from the box Billy offered her from the small table next to the bed.

"Zoey and I have always assumed you were born to Sanford and Belle. We didn't know anything about Gracie's part in your life until we were all in the living room looking at those pictures with you. That's when we knew, when we saw you sitting there on the sofa looking exactly like the Gracie we grew up with," Billy explained carefully.

Eva felt bad she had assumed Billy and Zoey had kept her in the dark. "I asked Mama and Daddy about her, about Gracie, and while Daddy was telling me how she gave her child away, I started to remember everything. I could see her so plain in my mind. How could I have forgotten all these years?"

"Well, baby, the mind is a funny thing. Sometimes it protects us by letting us remember only what we're able to handle at the time. Meanwhile, we grow and mature and get strong enough to deal with the tougher issues," Billy said, trying to help her understand.

Eva wished she could shake the anger she felt toward her parents but was unable to do so just yet. "How could Mama and Daddy have kept it from me? I deserved to know where I come from."

Billy waited a moment or two allowing Eva to sob and feel sorry for herself. She realized it was a crucial part of her being able to heal and move on.

"What you deserved was to have two parents that love you no matter what and that's, exactly what you have always had. Now maybe they were just trying to protect you and wanted to keep you safe and happy. Give you time to realize how loved you really are," Billy said when the time was right.

"What about Gracie? How could she give me up like that? I was her daughter and she let me go!" Eva wailed in response to the sharp pain piercing her heart.

Billy attempted to ease Eva's troubled mind. "Yes, you were, her daughter and she let you go because she too wanted to protect you. Don't you see? Gracie was young. She wasn't ready to raise a child but it, doesn't mean she didn't love you. She and her parents knew you could have a better life if you went to live with your daddy. Only love moves folks to make such a sacrifice as that."

Neither one spoke for a while. Billy wanted to give Eva time to think things over. "Guess I didn't look at it like that. I feel so bad I've been just awful to Mama and Daddy," Eva realized.

"I know your parents understand how you've been feeling because they're your parents and they love you. That's all there is to it. Beyond all of that, I need you to listen to me good now." Billy lifted Eva's chin to look her in the eye. "Sometimes it's harder to see what we *do* have, than it is to imagine what we *don't*. Now you keep that in mind, young lady."

Billy kissed Eva softly on the forehead and said a silent prayer that she would survive all that was ahead of her.

Eva's tears had shed their limit for the night and the aroma of zucchini oatmeal cookies wafted through the house, creating a sense of peace and tranquility.

"Are you ready to face the world now, hon?" Billy asked Eva tenderly.

"Yes, ma'am, I've got to stop being such a crybaby." Eva grinned, scolding herself as she dried her face with a tissue.

"There now, I know you're going to be all right because I can see a glimmer of that sense of humor you're always carrying around with you." Billy winked at her and they made their way out to join the others.

Sissy was still talking up a storm when they entered the kitchen. "...his name is Joe and he's so handsome you can't believe. Anyhow, he and Eva's in, love. You can tell by the kooky way they stare into one another's eyeballs."

"Sissy, I'm going to snatch you baldheaded for telling stories on me like that, you little bug! Ooooh," Eva rushed toward her with clenched fists and Sissy leaped from the counter, screeching at the top of her lungs as she scurried into the living room with Eva chasing her.

Zoey stood with her mitted chicken hands in the air looking bewildered at all the commotion. Billy followed the screaming banshees, cornering them in the living room just as Eva clenched a handful of Sissy's hair. Sissy continued to squeal with her eyes closed tight until she opened them to see Miss Billy glaring at them with the same expression their mama always used.

"We're so sorry, Miss Billy. I can't imagine what came over us." Eva was thoroughly embarrassed.

"Sorry." Sissy pulled her shirt down, as it had slid above her belly button during the struggle.

Billy held her posture, "I forgive you, under one condition," she bargained.

"Yes, ma'am," Eva was a little surprised she was making them work for it.

"I want to know all there is to know about this young man you have failed to tell me about while we carve our pumpkins and eat some cookies, deal?" Billy grinned.

"Yes, ma'am," Eva grinned back.

The three of them joined Zoey as she laid news papers on the floor setting a plate of cookies and a pitcher of cold milk on top of them so they could easily reach them while they carved. They each grabbed their chosen squash and sat to create the scariest faces they could think of. "Now be sure and save the seeds and we'll dry them in the oven to eat later." Zoey instructed them.

Billy cut the tops off of each one and the girls stuck their hands in to pull the slimy guts out then scraped the remains with a spoon. Billy raised one eyebrow at Eva. "Well child, let's hear it." She made her keep her promise as, she zig zagged a mouth onto the bright orange shell with a black Sharpie pen.

Eva blushed, but told the story about the boy who helped her bring her cow home. "Anyhow, he works at the mill with Daddy and Sissy's right, he *is* big and cute and he lives in town just over the hill from us."

"Well he can't be too close by, if he's living in town," Billy remarked, drawing the classic slanted eyes.

"He and his ma moved into the Henry place," Eva explained.

Zoey looked confused. "Well, isn't that strange? Why just today Polly said our Grac..."

"Zoey, we need more milk!" Billy exclaimed, intentionally interrupting her.

"Well, what in the world is the matter with you? We've got plenty of milk right here, Bill." Zoey picked up the pitcher to prove it was so.

Billy stared at Zoey with saucer eyes, not knowing what to say but wished she could tell her to keep her thoughts on the subject to herself.

Zoey scrunched her face at Billy. "Well, land sakes, I never." A knock at the door distracted her from finishing her sentence. "Well, who in the world," she stood to answer the door as a young, impetuous boy waited in the dark on the other side.

"Let me get it, Zoe." Billy wiped her hands on a towel and stepped in front of her when she remembered Manson had not yet been found. "Who is it?"

The young man cleared his throat. "Uh, my name's Joe, ma'am. I don't know if I'm at the right place or not but I'm looking for a Miss Eva?"

"Oh, *Miss* Eva, huh," Billy teased, while Zoey and Sissy chuckled.

"Yes, ma'am," he replied.

Eva's jaw hit the floor when Billy opened the door and she saw him waiting with his hands in his pockets.

"Joe? What are you doing here?" Eva giggled in her weird, new way.

"Come on in, boy, it's chilly out there." Billy held the screen door open and he stepped inside.

"Thank you, ma'am, I don't mean to interrupt, I just wanted to come and visit with Eva a spell if that's OK." He felt awkward now that he was there.

The four females ogled the handsome young man and Billy sat back down on the floor. "Name's Joe, you say? So this is your friend you've been telling us about, huh, Eva girl?" Billy teased.

Eva was twitter pated at the notion of him walking so far in the dark to see her. "Oh uh, yes, ma'am, it is."

"Been talking about me, huh?" He grinned mischievously.

Eva blushed, silently chiding herself for allowing him to take her breath away.

"Well have a seat, young man. Maybe Eva will let you help her carve out her Jack-o lantern," Zoey invited him.

"Thank you, ma'am, don't mind if I do," he politely accepted, sitting on the floor next to Eva.

Billy's mind raced, wondering that maybe Polly had been mistaken. After all, how in God's name could this white boy be Gracie's son?

"Hey, Joe," Sissy sang. She just couldn't keep from flirting with him.

"Hey, Sissy," He sang back, tweaking her nose.

Billy closed her gaping jaw when she realized she must be coming off rude. "Well, where are my manners? Nice of you to make the trip over here, how'd you find us?"

"Truth is, I went to Eva's house and spoke with her parents and they told me where she was. I decided to take a chance on getting here before it got dark but I didn't quite make it," he explained, stabbing a knife into one of the eyes Eva had drawn on her pumpkin.

Zoey poured him a tall glass of milk before offering him the red platter of warm cookies, scrutinizing every feature of his attractive face.

Joe laid the knife down and took a cookie. "Do I have mud on my face or something? I mean, you two haven't quit staring at me since I got here," he quipped jovially, wiping his cheek with his hand.

Zoey was flustered at his honesty and started rambling aimlessly. "Where are our manners? We didn't even introduce ourselves. I'm Zoey and this here's Billy. We've been friends of Eva's folks for years. Grew up together, you know, in school and all. Of course Billy's the oldest of all of us but still, we..."

"For Heaven's sake, Zoe, simmer down a notch or two. You can give him our names without revealing our shoe size, can't you?" Billy attempted to calm her down even though she knew it was too late to catch that horse.

"Nice to meet you both," Joe raised his eyebrows and winked discreetly at Eva, making her feel as though all her troubles were behind her now that he was there.

"You must be thinking we're loons or something. The truth is we're acting so nutty because Eva says you moved into the old Henry place but just today we heard our friend Gracie and her son had moved into that house and she's well, a little darker in color than you, is all. We must have misunderstood, huh, Bill?" Zoey looked at Billy for support but received a disapproving look instead.

Billy faded three shades and Eva furrowed her brow as she tried to make sense of what Zoey said.

Joe wanted to relieve the sudden tension in the room. "Yeah, I get that a lot. Fact is, even Mr. Johnson was surprised to find out I was my mother's son. Guess they knew each other pretty well when they were in school." Joe found it humorous that the color of his skin had such an effect on people.

Eva stiffened, unable to speak as Joe explained he had been adopted by Gracie when he was very young. Her skin grew hot as she pondered the notion that Gracie had given her up, only to adopt a child later and, furthermore, she had fallen hard for the boy who was in a roundabout way, family.

"*Gracie?* You mean she lives in town and she's...your mother? My father knew all along? So this is what Mama meant when she said we have a lot more to talk about!" Eva screamed, unnerving Joe.

Billy looked compassionately at Eva before jumping to the task of controlling the fires that kept flaring up around them. "Sissy girl, it's getting kind of late. Why don't you go on and brush your teeth before snuggling into your pj's? We'll tuck you in after bit, OK, Sugar?"

Sissy threw out her bottom lip in a dramatic pout but Billy responded with her powerful evil eye, cautioning her, to do as she was told. "Yes, ma'am," Sissy put the lid on her scowling pumpkin and stood obediently, quickly wiping her hands on the towel, "Night, everybody."

Joe looked perplexed and opened his mouth to speak when Eva dropped her spoon to the floor. "What's going on?" He was thoroughly confused.

Billy was furious with Zoey but softened when she saw her partner was wracked with guilt over speaking out of turn. "Eva, I think it's time you take Joe out to the porch and have a little talk, don't you?"

Eva looked at Billy with fear in her eyes. "But I..."

"The time has come, young lady. Don't make this nice young man continue to wonder what the heck is going on." Billy nudged her.

"Eva, what is it?" Joe felt awful when he saw how upset she was.

Eva shuddered, but stood to her feet and washed her hands at the kitchen sink. "Won't you come too, Miss Billy?" she asked, hopefully.

Billy remained in her seat. "I'm here if you find you need me but this is yours to handle as you wish, sweetheart. It's finally your turn to say how this is going to go."

Eva gained strength from Billy because she always had a way of offering a perspective on things she would never have thought of on her own.

"Come on, Joe, we need to talk," she said firmly, trying to control her nerves as she led him out the door.

A crocheted afghan hung on the back of the porch swing, so Joe wrapped it around Eva's shoulders before they sat down. "What is it, Eva? Why are you so upset?"

Eva wondered if he would still be so nice toward her once he heard what she was about to say. "I don't know how to begin, so I'm just going to say it."

"Well good, you know I don't want it any other way," he assured her.

Unable to face him, Eva stared out into the darkness. "I guess you already know, your mama and my daddy used to date when they, were young?" she began.

"Well, no. I mean, Ma said, they knew one another but she didn't say anything about them dating. Why? Does that bother you?" Joe felt she was overreacting.

"No. I mean, there's more to it than that," she continued.

"Well whatever it is, it can't be all that bad." He kissed the back of her hand tenderly.

Eva was overcome with attraction to him and found it difficult to pull away from his grasp. "I hope you still feel that way when I tell you what I've got to tell you."

He could see she was struggling to get the words out. "It's all right. I want you to trust me and just be honest about whatever it is."

Eva turned to face him and felt as if she were jumping off a cliff. "I'm, I'm your mother's daughter."

The words seemed to push him back against the swing. "What's that you say?" He considered she might be joking and waited for her to laugh but she was motionless, holding her breath. "You got me, very funny, very funny!" Eva was truly distressed and she looked like a scared little girl as she watched him laugh at her. "Wait a minute. What do you mean by that, Eva?" He suddenly saw his mother's features staring back at him.

She closed her eyes, praying for strength as the words came out more crudely than she had intended. "I mean that my daddy got your mama pregnant in high school and I'm the baby they made between them." She shrank.

He stood without taking time to think. "So you're telling me that you're my *sister*?" The vapor was thick when his warm breath met the brisk air and the veins in his temples pumped fervently. He hurried down the wooden steps, stopping at the bottom and turned to face her again, seeing the truth still staring back at him. "This can't be! My mother would have told me, right?"

"Wait, Joe," Eva cried.

"She would have told me!" He stormed out into the darkness.

Billy heard him yelling and stepped out to see if they were all right. "Joe! Come back, Joe! You'll be eaten alive for sure if you go walking in those woods this time of night. Let me take you home." Manson was the one beast she was most concerned about.

Joe felt embarrassed that he needed her help but he knew she was right and stomped to the driveway. Billy kissed Eva on the head on her way down the steps and unlocked the doors of the Scout to let Joe in. They drove away and Joe disappeared without the slightest glance back at the petrified girl he left frozen on the swing.

* * *

TWENTY-TWO

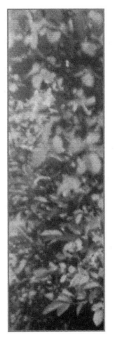

"Ma, wake up, Ma!" Joe yelled, when he entered the house fuming mad, slamming the door behind him. He and Billy had ridden in silence. She knew Joe needed space and time to think, but he became angrier at the duplicity he had unwittingly endured from his mother.

"What the hell are you yelling for?" Gracie groaned from her bed. Joe turned on the lamp and she yanked the blankets up over her head. He felt no sympathy for waking her when he saw the empty scotch glass and ashtray full of butts on the bedside table. "What the hell is wrong with you? *Please* go to bed and leave me be," she begged him.

"No, Ma. Neither one of us are going to sleep until I get some answers out of you," he demanded.

"Answers about what, boy? Leave it until morning." She wanted nothing more than for him to go away.

"Answers about a little girl you gave away long before you ever even thought of me," Joe declared boldly, not wanting to wait another moment to hear what she had to say about it.

Gracie pulled the blankets down slowly, rolling apprehensively to face him before sitting up to lean against the wrought iron headboard. Clearing her throat, she slowly, methodically, pushed the hair out of her eyes then slid a cigarette from its hard pack with the flip top and lit up, sucking the smoke down deep into her lungs. When the calming effects of the nicotine finally delivered the courage she needed, she waited for him to coax her a little bit more.

Joe glared at his mother. "Well? I hear you gave up a baby when you were young. Is that right?" he accused her.

Gracie took another drag before deciding to come clean. "Not exactly, she wasn't a baby when I let my parents give her to Sanford. I assume you know he's the father?" Joe nodded his head. "Anyhow, she was four years old."

"Four years old? Ma! How could you? How could you give Eva up at all but especially when she'd been with you for so long?" Thoughts of his own birth mother's decision to give him up when he was two played through his mind and he was dumbfounded that the woman who raised him could have done such a selfish thing.

"Listen, Joe. I was young and living kind of wild back then. I let my parents talk me into doing something I really didn't want to do but they convinced me it was the best thing for the child, for Eva," Gracie divulged feeling more embarrassed than regretful.

"If you were so wild and didn't want, any kids, why in God's name, did they let you adopt me? Don't they check people out before they go giving them babies?" he asked incredulously.

"Son, I wanted Eva, I did. I just wasn't ready to give her the kind of life she deserved. I ached for her from the moment my folks gave her away and I felt so empty inside. I suppose that's what moved me to adopt you, once I got out on my own. The agency had so many kids just getting older every year they were happy to let me bring you home. Being a mother to you made me feel whole again. You gave me a reason to settle down."

He thought about her words for a moment. "So you adopted me just so you could feel better about yourself. Is that it?"

"No, baby, you're taking it all wrong. Please listen to me." Gracie pleaded with him. "For years I didn't have any idea where Eva was and then about a year ago, I begged my ma to tell me and she finally admitted Eva was here in Stockton with Sanford. I've been trying to get us back to this boring town ever since. What I'm saying is, loving you and loving Eva have nothing to do with one another but I do love you both so much."

Joe paced the floor, considering her explanation.

"Why haven't you ever told me any of this? Especially now that we're here and you know I've fallen head over heels for Eva, for your daughter."

For the first time, Gracie showed a little humility. "Because I'm a coward, son, always have been, and I know it. I'm not proud of some of my decisions but they are what they are and there's no way to take them back."

He was touched by her humble attitude, as he had never known her to admit her weaknesses before. "When were you going tell me? I mean, there's no way I can go on feeling like I do about Eva now that I know these things."

Gracie straightened her posture and reached out to him. He had every reason to be skeptical about her motives but he accepted her hand before sitting beside her on the bed. "Listen to me, son. There's no reason you and Eva can't still make something together. It's not like you're blood. I mean you couldn't be further from it. Can't you see you're a white boy?" Gracie teased him, hoping he wouldn't be angry with her anymore.

He barely grinned and closed his eyes, trying to make sense of it all. "You really think so, Ma? I mean, it isn't too weird?" The anger and resentment he was so determined to hang on to only moments ago seemed to melt away.

"Well, I didn't say it wasn't weird," Gracie continued to humor him. "But I've never seen you act so gaga over a girl before. Don't let her go just because I screwed up a long time ago. I know what it's like to have something come between you and the one you love. Don't let it happen to you, son."

He knew she was right. "Truth is, Ma, the way I feel, I couldn't let her go if I tried."

Gracie hugged him tightly with a hint of desperation. "Please tell me you forgive me, son. I'll just die if you don't."

"I forgive you, Ma, but it may take me awhile to understand why you kept this from me." He was candid with his mother. Gracie shut her eyes tight, silently thanking God above that her son had found it in his heart to show her mercy. Joe kissed her on the cheek and turned off her light before going to his own room and crawling into bed. He couldn't sleep as his mind replayed the way he had left things with Eva. "I'm such a jerk!" He landed a fist into his pillow.

He was tempted to call her, but realized it was the middle of the night and continued to worry what she must think of him. He couldn't help but wish he had handled everything so differently and considered what he could have done, what he *should* have done as the clock continued to tock at three o'clock in the morning. He knew he would be worth very little at work if he didn't get some shut-eye and he finally drifted off to sleep around four fifteen, only to have the alarm wake him at six. The sound of it buzzed and sliced through his pounding skull like the saw he ran at the mill. Reluctantly, he tumbled out of bed still wearing his clothes from the night before.

Stumbling into the living room, he quickly put on his jacket, grabbed his gloves and boots and headed out the door, not bothering to eat breakfast. He wasn't able to stomach any food after the long night of much-deserved suffering. He sat on the front stoop to put on his boots, expecting the crisp air to help clear his head but he choked on smoke instead, and noticed it was billowing out the open door of Polly's fabric store.

"Oh dear lord," Joe rushed into his mother's bedroom, shaking her in an attempt to wake her up. "Ma, call the fire department!"

Clueless and dead to the world, she moaned and flopped onto her back, responding with a resonant snore. He gave up and went to the telephone to call them himself before racing outside and down the street toward Polly's. Flames danced in and out of the shop and he used his light jacket in a futile attempt to beat the life out of them.

Wailing sirens pierced the silence as curious onlookers lined the streets, shivering in their robes and flannel pajamas, hoping to catch a glimpse of the fascinating crime scene.

A fireman pulled Joe out of the way as his fellow workers attached cumbersome hoses to the truck and cranked the wheel, releasing a deluge onto the blaze, hoping to save the small business from further destruction.

A policeman questioned Joe as Polly arrived to open the shop like any other work day, then rushed from her car, bawling out loud.

"Yes, Officer, I saw smoke and noticed the door was wide open but by the time I got here, the flames had taken over." Joe's head was spinning from utter exhaustion and fatigue, mixed with shock and wonder at who could have done such a thing. "Anything else I can do?" he offered.

"Nope, you can go, but we'll be giving you a call if we need anything else from you," the officer promised.

Joe had never officially met Polly, but he knew she was a single mother with two teenage daughters and he felt terrible about her misfortune. He didn't quite know what to say as he approached her. "I'm sure sorry about all of this, ma'am. I've got to get to work right now but if there's anything I can do, you let me know. I live just down the street there." He pointed at his house.

Polly barely nodded her head, numb from the shock of seeing her dream and livelihood going up in smoke.

Joe wished he could stay and help but turned to leave. He knew he should run because he was already late for work but he couldn't convince his legs to do as they should. Treading ponderously through the crowded streets, he was amazed at the number of people wrapped in blankets, sitting in lawn chairs, drinking their cups of coffee as if watching an early episode of *Matlock* on their television sets. He noticed the void on his own stoop. "Yep, Ma could sleep through a train wreck," he mused. His attention was drawn to one other empty porch but only one, where a pudgy-faced man watched from the narrow opening of the curtains inside. "Am I mistaken, or is that man laughing?"

* * *

TWENTY-THREE

Dear Billy and Zoey,
I'm glad to hear you two are doing so well. I haven't written in a while because I needed some time to think. Now that I know Blue and Sanford are married, I've decided to stay where I am for a while. I think it's best if you don't tell her you heard from me, I don't want to cause any trouble for them and their children.

I know she's just the best mother in the whole wide world. She and Sanford were always such good friends.

Hazel has taught me how to do pottery. I've made all sorts of things I didn't even know I had in me to do. I also enjoy helping out on the farm and Harold has been teaching me to ride horses. At the end of each day, I read stories, mostly ones written by Mark Twain of course. The other day we went into town and the Montgomery's showed me the house Sam Clemens actually lived in for many years. It was just amazing to know I was walking the halls of such a famous author. I have learned so much, my whole world has opened up. I feel like I'm part of something special here with these kind folks and I somehow know I'm where I'm supposed to be for now but I will never be whole without Blue.

We plan to go to Branson for the Ozark Mountain Christmas celebration a few days after Thanksgiving. The Montgomery's go every year in memory of their son, as it was a family tradition when he was alive.

To tell the truth, I would rather die than spend another holiday without Blue. All these years, I've dreamed of the day I would be free of my folks and spending my life with her. Anyhow, I'm glad to have something to keep me busy and my mind off what could have been.

Any sign of Manson on that end? I'm still waiting on pins and needles to know what's going to happen to me.

Love to you both,
Ronny Jean

* * *

TWENTY-FOUR

The smell of scrambled eggs, fried ham and strong coffee filled the house when Sanford came downstairs to find Belle in the kitchen making breakfast. He couldn't help but stare when he saw her dressed in a white, long sleeved thermal shirt, blue jeans, and a red hooded sweat jacket that zipped up the front. Despite all that had happened the day before, she looked radiant and well rested.

"Morning, Belle," he greeted her cheerfully.

"Morning, Sanford. What would you think about walking over to Billy's place to get the girls, instead of calling them on the phone?"

"Well now, that would be quite a surprise for the ladies of the house, wouldn't it? They haven't seen you in a coon's age," Sanford replied.

"No, Sanford, they haven't and I'm ashamed to admit it. I should have been over there a long time ago," Belle said, regretfully.

"Let's do it, then. It's a lovely day for a walk around the lake." Sanford opened the front door, letting fresh air into the house.

"All right, let's eat and get on our way." Belle set two plates of food on the table and a stack of buttered toast.

Sanford couldn't keep his eyes off of her. "You look like the girl we all used to know, Belle, simply beautiful yet sensational."

"God knows I'm finally comfortable for the first time in a long while too," Belle admitted, heaping a spoonful of eggs onto her slice of toast and jelly.

When they finished eating and clearing the table, they stepped out onto the porch. Sanford lit his pipe and took Belle's hand before starting down the path.

"How I love the colors of the leaves on the trees this time of year." Sanford tried to make conversation but Belle didn't reply. She was enjoying the beautiful scenery, the crisp air, and her new-found freedom. She no longer felt obligated to make idle conversation. Her thoughts were on the future. As the sun rose higher, the temperature did too so she removed her jacket, tying the sleeves around her waist.

They were a little surprised at how quiet it was when they arrived at Billy and Zoey's house. They laughed when they saw the half carved pumpkins, one sitting on each step. One had only one eye carved out with the other still waiting to be, and one had only half a jagged mouth and the other two had no triangle noses. They decided it made the faces look even scarier.

"Guess they didn't have time to finish these, huh?" Belle giggled and knocked lightly, hoping not to wake anyone who, might still be sleeping.

"Maybe we should have called first," Sanford whispered.

Billy opened the door and screamed at the vision of Sanford and Belle standing in front of her. "Holy Ghost, am I dreaming? Is it really you, Belle girl?"

"Yes, Billy woman, it's me." Belle smiled weakly when she noticed the gray peppering Billy's hair, blatantly reminding her of how long she had neglected her dear friends. Suffering the stab wounds of guilt, she searched Billy's eyes, hoping to see the face of forgiveness looking back at her.

Billy grabbed Belle and held her close as the childhood memories of days gone by filled their minds and flooded their hearts. Zoey came from the bedroom, still wearing her robe and squealed when she saw the couple standing in the doorway. She leaped onto Sanford, hugging him tightly around the neck as Belle and Billy held each other, laughing through the tears when they saw the frightened expression on Sanford's face.

"Come in and have some coffee, you two, we've got loads to talk about." Billy squeezed Belle's hand and led her into the living room, determined to never let her go and Sanford followed them.

Zoey took her turn at hugging Belle. "You're going to have to share her a minute, Bill. You're looking good, girl, look at you in your blue jeans. Now that's the Belle we know and love." She winked and went to the kitchen to gather a red carafe' shaped like a rooster and four coffee cups that resembled nesting hens.

"Isn't she something, Zoe? Our girl is back and we have missed her so," Billy said, as she and Belle took a seat on the sofa.

"It's so quiet around here you wouldn't even know there were kids in the house," Sanford joked, sitting in the recliner that faced the sofa and love seat.

"Oh, the girls are still sleeping. We were all up pretty late last night." Zoey set the tray down, feeling embarrassed over her part in the chaotic evening before.

Steaming hot coffee flowed from the rooster's beak, as Billy filled each guest's cup and Belle sensed uneasiness from her friends. "How'd it go? Did they give you any trouble?"

The ladies of the house glanced at one other and Billy set her cup down on the saucer that was painted to look like hay.

"Belle, Sanford, we had quite a night. The girls were lovely as always but I'm afraid we opened a hornet's nest," Billy began. "That boy came over last night. You know, Gracie's boy," she finished in a soft mutter, looking down at the floor.

"What the devil was he doing over here? I told him not to come." Sanford said a little too loudly.

Belle hushed him, trying to think. "OK, so what happened?"

"So you know the boy is Gracie's son, then?" Billy knew the answer before she even asked the question.

"Of course, Bill. Hell has turned the demons loose at our house. Just tell us what happened and don't hold back."

Belle braced herself for the worst.

Billy told the twisted chain of events from the day they gave Eva the photo album and noticed the resemblance between her and Gracie, to their trip to Polly's when they discovered Gracie was back in town.

"Anyhow, the boy left Eva here with a broken heart and crying herself to sleep last night," Billy concluded.

Sanford clenched his fists. "I'm going to whoop him."

Belle understood how Sanford felt and tried to calm him down. "Listen, Sanford, think of Joe's part in this. He's young and he must have been confused out of his mind just like Eva was when she learned about Gracie being her blood mama."

Sanford softened. "You're right, Belle. I'll go and talk to Joe. Matter of fact, why don't I go now and let you girls catch up?"

"You all right, Sanford?" Belle knew he may have reached his limit of tolerance.

"I'm fine, Belle, there just has to be an end to all of this somewhere, you know? You take care of our girls when they wake up and I'll see you all at home later on." He stood to leave and Belle walked him to the door, giving him a hug.

Zoey suddenly piped up. "Please forgive me for blabbing. I feel just awful," she purged, as she ran to hug them both.

Sanford and Belle felt sympathy toward their agonizing friend, and the three of them hugged one other as Billy watched, happy to be reunited again.

"These things happen the way they do for a reason." Sanford wanted to ease her worried mind.

"That's right, Zoe. You did nothing wrong. Truth be told, you made the load lighter for us. We didn't know how we were going to tell Eva on top of everything else so I suppose we should be thanking you for doing it for us." Belle comforted her.

"It's all going to be just fine" Sanford reassured her and kissed her on the forehead before heading out the door.

* * *

TWENTY-FIVE

"Boy! You're looking like hell today!" Sanford yelled over the grind of the saw.

Joe barely noticed him through the thick of the blinding sawdust and turned to feed another log onto the carriage when Sanford stepped closer.

"Sanford?" he acknowledged him feebly, not knowing what to say or where to even begin.

"Come here, son. I told Mr. Farnsworth I was going to buy you a cup of coffee." Sanford patted him on the shoulder.

Joe lifted his goggles to sit on the top of his head and they went to the break room, where Sanford plugged the vending machine with dimes. Joe sat down heavily at the filthy table with sticky rings of soda pop and newspapers strewn all over.

"I hear you had quite a time last night." Sanford handed him a cardboard cup filled with something black and way too thick to be good coffee.

Joe set the cup on the table, rubbing his bloodshot eyes. "You're right about that."

"What's on your mind, son? Are you mad? Frustrated, plain confused? Talk to me." Sanford could see he was genuinely oppressed.

Joe stared blankly at the wall. "What can I say? I'm falling for your daughter... you and my mother's daughter, and I'm, just not sure that's OK. I don't know where to take it from here but I do know I hate the way I left things with Eva last night and I don't know how to go about telling her so."

Sanford listened patiently, feeling sympathy for the young, man. "It's unfortunate you found out the way you did. That was the fault of your mother and me. I guess I liked you from the start and knowing you and Eva could end up being a couple pleased me so I didn't see any reason to cause a fuss."

Joe was a little surprised Sanford felt that way. "You don't, see anything wrong with us being together?"

"Not in the least bit. You're not blood. Hell, you weren't even raised together like step siblings. You're just two young people who care an awful lot for each other and the way you two came together could be looked at as a miracle." Sanford hoped to give him a more positive perspective on the situation.

Joe sat quietly, letting the notion sink in. "I do feel something real for Eva and I can't keep my mind on anything else since I ran out on her last night. I was scared to death to think I might be in love with my own sister and angry at my ma for not telling me when she knows how much Eva means to me."

"I understand, son, and if you tell her like you just told me, Eva will too. Take it from someone who knows, that girl has a way of forgiving easily." Sanford stood to leave, and they shook hands. "You need to get some rest tonight, boy. I've never seen you so low."

"Once I speak with Eva I'm sure I'll sleep like a rock. Will you tell her I'll be giving her a call after work tonight? I need to stay a little longer to make up for being late this morning," he replied.

Sanford knew Joe would never be late without having a good reason. "I know you're upset about Eva and all, but being late for work just doesn't sound like you."

"Oh, I was up in time to get here but the fire at Polly's place was what made me so late. Mr. Farnsworth understands, but I don't want my paycheck hurting come payday is all," he explained.

Sanford was shocked at the unexpected news. "The hell you say? There was a fire at Polly's?"

"Oh, yes, sir. I saw the smoke when I came out of my house this morning and the funny thing was the door was hanging wide open. That's why the police think it may be arson," Joe explained further.

"Anybody hurt?" Sanford wondered about Polly.

"Didn't seem to be, at first I was worried Miss Polly might be inside but she didn't get there until later. Anyhow, I better run. Tell Eva I'll call her, won't you Sanford?"

"I sure will, we'll see you now," Sanford promised. He headed for town to check out the situation and wanted to see how Polly was doing, thinking of the events of the last few days along the way. He smiled when he thought about Eva and Sissy sleeping comfortably as Belle caught up on old times with Billy and Zoey. When he drove past Gracie's house, he decided he would stop by and see what she was up to once he knew Polly was all right.

Yellow caution tape stretched across the door of the fire-damaged storefront and Sanford could see Polly sorting through the damaged goods as he parked in front of the building. He was stunned as he walked inside and saw all the ash and destruction around him. "Pol," he addressed her softly, not wanting to startle her.

Polly whirled around glad to see her old friend. "Sanford? Who would do such a thing? I can't believe it. The police were here investigating as if it was done on purpose but they didn't find anything." She bawled, throwing her arms around his neck.

"I'm so sorry this happened, Pol. What can I do to help you?" Sanford wished he could take all her troubles away.

"I don't know, San. I guess I just have to muddle through all this mess. I can't save anything because it all smells like smoke and what didn't burn was ruined by all the water from the hoses." Polly sobbed, feeling hopeless.

Sanford thought for a moment. "Tell you what, Pol. I'll see if Belle can bring the girls tomorrow to come and help you. I have to work but I'll talk to the guys at the mill and we'll do any heavy lifting that needs to be done, put new linoleum on these floors and paint the walls with a special kind of paint that covers up the smell of smoke too. By the time we're done, you'll never know there was a fire in this place and you can start fresh."

Polly was overcome with gratitude and hugged him again, adding a tender kiss on the cheek.

Gracie stood watching them from the doorway and it was clear she wasn't there to help Polly. She was wearing an emerald green suit jacket with black cuffs and a black stand up collar. Three black buttons ran down the bodice and stopped at her waist to show off her black leather mini skirt, sheer black stockings and trademark black high heels. "Well, well, well. Looks like a party," she sneered.

Polly didn't pull away from Sanford. "Hey, Gracie, what can I do for you? As you can see, we're closed for business today."

Sanford kept his arms wrapped around Polly. "Hey, Gracie, I came to see what I can do to help Polly out here. Can you believe anyone would do such a terrible thing?" he asked incredulously.

Gracie crossed her arms in front of her. "No, I can't. I'm sorry it happened, Polly."

"Thank you, Gracie. Well, I suppose I best get back to it, then." Polly turned from Sanford's embrace and he squeezed her hand before turning her loose.

"OK, then, I'll get everybody rounded up and Belle will be here to help you out first thing tomorrow morning," Sanford promised.

"Sanford, thank you again. You have a way of making me feel like everything's going to be all right." Polly tried to smile wishing he didn't have to go.

"It is Pol, don't you worry. Why don't you go home and try to get some rest?" Sanford suggested.

"Maybe I should. I'm so exhausted I can't even think straight." Polly dropped the broom she was holding and Sanford and Gracie followed her out the door.

They waved good-bye to one another. Polly got into her car, Sanford into his truck, and Gracie walked down the sidewalk toward her house. As soon as Polly had driven out of sight, Sanford got out of his truck and met Gracie, who was waiting around the corner of the building with her arms crossed, tapping her toe impatiently, as if he were a child about to get a spanking.

"You coming over to play or not," She pouted.

"I was planning on doing so." He grinned.

"Well, all right, then, let's go home." She turned on her heel, waggling her finger over her shoulder.

Sanford followed her down the street and into her house, closing the door behind him. Gracie turned and pinned him against the door with her petite form. "Saw you drive by earlier, I was thinking maybe you had better things to do than me and there I found you in the arms of another woman." She flirted with him.

Sanford grew hot, reeling from the pressure of Gracie's body crushed against his. "It's only you, Gracie, it's always been you."

She barely grazed her ruby red lips against his and said with but a whisper, "Oh yeah? Prove it."

And he did.

* * *

TWENTY-SIX

As they laughed and reminisced Belle studied her old school chums who were a bit more wrinkled around the edges than they used to be but the young girls within, were still the same.

"Truly, Belle, you just look wonderful. You and Sanford seem so happy too," Zoey declared.

Billy drank her last sip of coffee. "She's right, Belle you do look good. I don't know how you were able to stand wearing your mother's old dresses choking the life out of you all that time. Hmmph! You hated all that falderal when you, were a little girl. I knew you couldn't have liked it any better as a grown woman."

"You're so right, I was suffocating." Belle shook her head wondering how she put up with it all those years.

"When did you take to wearing your jeans again?" Zoey asked.

"Only this morning, matter of fact, and just to make this perfectly clear, the reason Sanford and I look so happy together is because, well, we've decided to part." Belle didn't quite know how else to say it.

"The hell you say, girl?" Billy exclaimed.

"It's true. You know we've been living a lie all these years as husband and wife, so we think maybe it's time to part and start living the truth as friends. I feel like I'm starting my life over again and, to tell you the truth, it feels pretty good," Belle said confidently.

"Well, I'll be," Zoey gaped. "You know I love Sanford like a brother but I just never could imagine you ever being with a well, you know." Zoey wrinkled her nose, "A *man* all these years, Belle, even if it was our Sanford!" They all laughed at that.

"Well, beyond what it took to bring Sissy into this world, there wasn't much of that kind of being together, if you know what I mean," Belle explained. "And when there was, I was just going through the motions trying to convince even myself that I should be someone different than I really am I guess."

"Now, Belle, what do you mean you're going to part? Do you mean you're getting a divorce or what?" Billy asked.

Belle considered the lengthy conversation she and Sanford had only the day before. "I suppose there's no reason for hiding it since you already know Gracie's back in town. She and Sanford found one another again, so we don't really know if he's going to be staying at the house or what's going to come of it. We'll just see how it all goes, and will try to do what's best for the girls."

Billy and Zoey gasped at the juicy news about Sanford and Gracie.

"You don't mean he, and Gracie...?" Zoey began naively, but couldn't bring herself to say the words out loud.

"Yes, Zoe, that's what she means," Billy confirmed.

"Belle, darling, didn't it just crush you to find out about it?" Zoey asked, holding her hand to her heart.

Belle searched for the right words. "No, I can't say it did. The best way, I can explain it is, hearing him say he'd moved on made me feel I was finally free to do the same. It gave me permission to be myself again."

Billy looked tenderly at her born-again friend. "Oh, Belle, we have no idea what you've been through, do we?"

"I've been doing what I felt I had to do, but all the pretending has run its course. If I was ever so blessed as to find my Ronny, I'd run into her arms so fast..." She paused to choke down the tears, imagining the possibility.

Zoey's lips were puckered as she struggled to hold the words in her mouth like a dam bracing a waterfall. Billy knew what she was thinking and nervously bit a hangnail on her thumb, wondering what to do.

"Belle, there's something we've been meaning to tell you," Billy began.

Zoey brightened, knowing Billy was going to reveal the letters from Ronny.

"Mama," Eva and Sissy meandered into the living room, rubbing the sleep from their eyes, each competing for a spot on Belle's lap.

"Good morning darlings. How did you sleep, huh?" Belle hugged them close.

"Good." Sissy yawned. "You look different, Mama, real pretty."

"Well thank you, sugar." Belle noticed Eva's swollen eyes and tear-stained cheeks. "You've had a load of unexpected news lately, haven't you, honey?"

"Yeah, Mama," Eva agreed somberly as Belle stroked her hair.

Belle tried to comfort her oldest who had been forced to grow up so quickly since her last birthday. "Listen, baby, your father and I were going to talk to you today about Joe and Gracie and all, but I guess it just wasn't meant to go that way."

Zoey noticed Sissy squirming around, trying to get comfortable as Belle rocked the chair gently back and forth hoping to help Eva relax.

"Come here, little one, you're about to wear your clothes clean through! Now why don't we go into the kitchen and see if we can rustle up some breakfast. Sound like a plan?" Zoey held out her hand for Sissy to take.

Sissy carelessly leaped from Belle's lap and Eva made a face at her sister but was too depressed to yell at her like she normally would.

"You think he'll ever want to see me again, Mama?" Eva asked after many moments of silence.

Belle laid her cheek on the top of Eva's head. "He's a good man and you're a wonderful young lady so I'm sure he will, baby. Matter of fact, your daddy's gone to the mill to have a little talk with him."

Eva bolted upright, making Belle's head jerk backward. "What? Mama, no! I could die, I could just die!" Eva screamed, jumping off her lap to face her.

Belle remembered what it was like to be a teenage girl embarrassed by everything coming and going but seeing her Eva act that way was going to take some getting used to.

"I understand how you're feeling, but you're going to have to trust your daddy to take care of this. After all, he's partly responsible, isn't he?" Belle tried to sympathize with her.

"But Joe will never want to speak to me again, never!" Belle and Billy watched as Eva stomped her foot and blew out of the room in a huff before slamming the bedroom door behind her.

Belle was stunned at her daughter's disrespectful behavior. "Well, that didn't go as smoothly as I'd hoped. What in the world has come over her?"

Billy raised her eyebrows at Belle. "Seriously, Belle, think about what that girl has been through lately. Mix all of that into a big bowl of teenage hormones and attitude and you're bound to have an explosion from time to time."

Belle looked at Billy like she had just said something monumental and they broke into a hearty guffaw just like old times, whining the last of the belly laugh in unison.

"Hey, you were going to tell me something when the girls came in. What was it?" Belle reminded her.

Billy decided to postpone showing Belle the letters until a time when there would be no distractions.

"Oh uh, you and the girls want to join us for Thanksgiving? Sanford's welcome too, but sounds like he may have other plans by then," she quickly improvised.

"I don't really know what Sanford's plans are, but you know the girls and I would love to come, Bill, thank you. So, that's it? Seemed like, you were going to say something much more serious than that," Belle added.

"Breakfast is served!" Sissy yelled from the kitchen.

Billy was glad for the interruption. "Well, we best get in there and eat something. I'm nearly starved to death!"

* * *

TWENTY-SEVEN

Belle and the girls were already home when Sanford pulled into the drive at six thirty. He had barely slipped out Gracie's back door before Joe came home from work.

"Hey there, how's, my best girls doing?" Sanford gave each one a kiss on the cheek, looking happier than he had in years.

"Daddy," Sissy squealed, returning the kiss and warming his heart.

Eva gave Sanford the cold shoulder and continued to set the table.

"Well, what in the world is the matter with you? Seems to me you'd, want to hug your old dad for working things out with your boyfriend." He thought she would be happy.

"This is all, your fault anyhow!" Eva screamed, rushing down the hallway to the security of her bedroom.

Sanford wasn't used to her speaking to him that way and the smile fell from his face.

Belle was filling the kitchen sink with hot soapy water. "Don't worry about it, Sanford. She's been this way all day. Guess we thought it would never happen to us, huh?"

"What's happened? It's like she's a different person." Sanford felt as though she had slapped him across the face.

Belle dried her hands on a dishtowel. "It's called puberty. Your baby girl is growing up. Besides, it's only natural she would be taking her anger out on us, San. We're the cause of a lot of her grief and now there's a boy involved. She *is* a teenage girl after all."

Sanford felt terrible. "But I thought she had decided to forgive us and all was well."

"That was *before* she found out her boyfriend has the same mother as she does." Belle sighed, tired of calling Gracie Eva's mother and wanted badly to change the subject. "So how'd it go, Sanford?" Belle was hoping to hear about his talk with Joe.

Sanford had just come from a torrid afternoon of romping in the love nest with Gracie and was astonished Belle wanted to know about it. "Huh? What?"

"Joe. You did talk to him, didn't you?" Belle asked, bursting his bubble.

That made much more sense to Sanford. "Oh! Yes, of course I did. He's head over heels for Eva and he's going to call her tonight to tell her so. That's what I wanted to tell her just now, before she yelled at me."

Eva could hear her parents talking and her spirit soared as she waited expectantly for the phone to ring.

"Eva! We're about to eat, girl! Are you going to join us?" Belle shouted down the hallway.

"No thank you, Mama! I'm doing my homework and I'm not hungry!" She hollered back, sounding slightly more civil than she had only moments ago.

Sissy finished setting the table and the three of them sat down as Sanford folded his hands to pray.

"Sanford, I think from now on we can all pray in our own way, in our own time." Belle reminded him, that things were changing fast in their household.

Sissy couldn't believe her ears and dove hungrily into the plate of fried catfish and mashed potatoes and gravy.

"Uh uh, little girl, you still have to eat your salad first," Belle instructed her youngest.

Sissy grinned wryly, as if she had almost gotten away with something naughty and bit into a carrot.

"Belle, there's something I need to talk to you about. Did you hear about Polly's place?" Sanford sounded morose.

"Polly's, no what's happened?" she asked.

"Joe says he saw it first thing this morning. He's the one who called the fire department, matter of fact. Apparently somebody set fire to her shop and she's having a real hard time. I said I'd see what kind of help you could round up for her in the morning," he explained.

Belle could hardly believe it. "Oh, Sanford, Is she all right? She's not hurt, is she?"

"No, no. It happened in the early morning when she wasn't there but she's pretty shook up about it, so I told her to go home and get some sleep."

"Oh, thank goodness! Who would do that to poor Polly? She's one of the nicest people I know. I bet Zoey doesn't know either. Of course we'll help her." Belle's mind was racing as she rushed to the telephone to call Billy and Zoey.

Sanford spread honey butter onto his warm cornbread. "OK, I knew you would. I'm going to get some guys to come and do what we can as far as painting and all, whatever it takes to get her back in business."

Zoey and Billy were shocked to hear the news and they both agreed to help out the next morning.

Belle hung up the phone and returned to the dinner table but had lost her appetite. "I'm going to keep the girls home from school so they can help too. Billy said they'll pick us up on their way into town."

"Sounds good, Belle," Sanford replied.

"Sissy, when you finish eating, girl, you need to get to bed. We're going to be getting up early," Belle instructed her.

"Yes, Mama," Sissy replied, glad she didn't have to go to school the next day.

Eva tried to be worried for Polly, but was too distracted by the telephone that wasn't ringing. How could she have known the minute Joe got home from work he passed out, thoroughly exhausted with nothing left to give.

* * *

TWENTY-EIGHT

Sanford had already left for work when Billy and Zoey knocked on the door early the next morning.

"Come in and have a cup of coffee. We're almost ready to go," Belle invited them.

"We just can't get over the news, Belle. I tried calling Polly last night but she didn't answer. You think she's all right?" Zoey wiped her feet on the mat before entering the house.

Belle took their jackets. "Yeah, Zoe, I'm sure she's fine. Sanford sent her home yesterday to get some sleep and she probably did just that." They all took a seat at the kitchen table just as Eva and Sissy entered the room, each one wearing old coveralls. Eva was depressed over not hearing from Joe like she had hoped to.

"Why in the world are we always the last to know what's going on? If we had known sooner, we could have been there for her when she may have needed us most." Zoey sounded frustrated.

"That's just one of the drawbacks of living in the backwoods and not having televisions to see the news, Zoe. I'm sure she needs us much more today, when we can really do something to help," Billy said.

"Morning, Mama, Miss Billy, Miss Zoey," Sissy greeted them with good manners.

"Good morning, girls," they replied in unison.

Eva barely smiled.

Belle poured hot coffee into Billy and Zoey's cups. "Eva, Sissy, sit down and have something to eat. I'm afraid we're going to be working hard today."

"You're being awful responsible going to Miss Polly's to help out, you know," Billy remarked sweetly to them, hoping to raise Eva's spirits.

Sissy smiled through a mouthful of eggs and Eva said, "Yes, ma'am."

Belle was frustrated with Eva's bad manners but she knew her friends understood. "Can I fix you ladies a plate?" Belle offered them.

"No, no, Zoey made us some flapjacks, Belle, but thanks just the same." Billy sipped the coffee Belle had intentionally made a little stronger than usual. "Mm, that coffee tastes good. It's downright chilly out there."

When the girls were finished eating, they stacked their plates in the sink. "Let's leave them for later and get on over to Polly's," Belle said, putting on her jacket.

Embracing Blue

Billy helped Zoey on with hers and they stepped outside, piling into the Scout. They drove through the woods and, finally pulled up in front of the fabric store. The horrific damage that had been done to the once bright and cheery shop made them wince. "What in the world are we going to say when we see Polly?" Zoey cried.

Billy opened her door then paused for a moment when she noticed how hurt Zoey was over seeing their dear friend's loss. "There's nothing we can say, Zoey girl. That's why we're here to help out. Doing, instead of talking, is the only way we can make a real difference for her."

They approached the storefront reverently, as if walking into a funeral home and saw Polly pushing black water from the front of the store, out the back door with a broom.

Without hesitation the loyal friends sloshed through the water toward her and Polly cried as Zoey held her in her arms. "We are going to get through this together, Pol. You aren't alone." Zoey hoped her words would give Polly strength.

"I know, Zoe, I know. Thank you all for coming. I just don't know where to begin." Polly continued to cry, feeling completely overwhelmed.

"Well, why don't we start where we are," Belle advised. "You just tell us what needs to be done and we'll see to it."

Polly pulled a tissue from inside her sleeve and blew her nose. "All right then, all the fabrics are done for. Some of the packaged stuff might be saved, but otherwise the rest has got to go straight to the dump." She shook her head disbelievingly.

Billy hoped suggesting a plan would help calm Polly. "You have insurance, don't you? Let's get some pictures of the damage and turn them in to your insurance company so you can file a claim."

Polly wiped her eyes and blew her nose again before taking a deep breath. "Oh my goodness, Billy, I've been so upset, I never even thought about that. Thank you! I'll get the camera." She relaxed a little bit now that she was surrounded by friends who offered hope. "One thing the fire didn't get to was the coffee pot. How about I brew some up? I think maybe I have some cocoa mix for you girls, if you'd like some."

Eva and Sissy accepted the offer gratefully, thinking maybe a cup of chocolate would make the work go a lot easier.

Polly got the coffee brewing then started taking pictures. The others cleaned up behind her, starting with the soggy bolts of fabric that needed to be hauled out to the trailer hooked to the back of Billy's Scout.

"You two get that end, please," Belle instructed Eva and Sissy, lifting one end of a heavy fabric bolt.

Billy and Zoey grabbed opposite ends of another and the women worked hard for hours until the trailer was loaded to its fullest capacity.

"That's all we're going to fit in there for now, Pol. Why don't we stack these others by the door? That way we can load them up this afternoon when we get back from the dump," Billy suggested.

"Then we can start wiping down the walls before Sanford and his crew, come in to paint," Belle added.

"That makes sense to me. I think it will be about time for a lunch break after that. My treat, of course," Polly replied, forcing the last of the water out the back door.

"I wish we would have thought to bring some fans with us to help dry this place up." Zoey wondered where they might get some from town.

"I've got two fans at my place." A familiar voice from the past offered from the front of the store. Gracie stood smoking a cigarette, dressed in creased jeans, a moss green sweatshirt, and high heels. "Thought I'd come by to see what I could do to help out."

The others were speechless, staring at the brazen feline. Eva recognized her right away and ran to hide in the break room with Sissy following close behind, wanting to comfort her older sister.

Billy marched assertively up to Gracie, standing so close Gracie tottered, almost falling off her elevated shoes. "Well, don't this, beat all. What in the hell do you think you're doing here?"

Gracie stepped back a bit, then, deliberately exhaled smoke into Billy's face. "Well, I've come to see what I can do to help Polly. Is that a crime?" She smiled sweeter than homemade molasses.

Billy rolled her sleeves and clenched her fists as if she were gearing up to punch Gracie in the eye. "Don't try to tell me you didn't see Belle and the girls loading the trailer."

"Well isn't this a fine howdy do, after all these years?" Gracie pouted, pretending to have her feelings hurt.

"We're glad to see you, Gracie, but we know you have a way of being sneaky when it comes to getting what you want," Billy expounded.

Gracie grinned, taking Billy's insult as a compliment, "Now, what could I possibly want Bill?"

Belle was watching from the back of the store, "It's all right, Billy. Time we got this out of the way anyhow."

Polly was still ignorant to the situation and couldn't believe Billy's behavior toward Gracie but knew she wouldn't be acting that way without good reason.

Gracie batted her eyelashes as she often did. "Why, I don't know what you mean. What is it we've got to get out of the way, Belle?"

"Hey, Gracie, don't you think there might have been a better way of doing this?" Belle approached her, trying to remain rational for Eva's sake.

Gracie's shoulders slumped and her demeanor softened once she decided to be honest. "To tell you the truth, I didn't know *how* to do it. I saw all of you coming in and out of the store here and I just couldn't resist coming over to see..."

Belle heaved a heavy sigh and put one hand on Gracie's shoulder. "Gracie, I swear to God above, you have never had a thought for anyone but yourself. How do you think you're making Eva feel right now? Huh?"

She hung her head, fidgeting with the chipped paint on her fingernail, as Belle scolded her like a child.

"Guess I didn't, think anything about it. I just knew I needed to see her, is all," Gracie admitted.

"Mama," Eva cried, stepping out from the back room.

Gracie immediately brightened and rushed toward the young girl with open arms, "Baby, my baby!" she gushed, attempting to embrace her.

Eva was frightened and ran to Belle, seeking security, "Mama!"

Gracie's heart dropped as she stood with empty arms she had mistakenly hoped Eva would be willing to fill. When she saw the embrace between Eva and Belle, she wanted to cry, but puffed out her chest instead and sauntered to the front door, breezing past the two without a word.

"Gracie," Belle said softly.

Gracie stopped in her tracks and closed her eyes, beseeching the holy ones to grant her courage. She turned around slowly to face the mother and daughter.

"Gracie, this is Eva...Eva, this is Gracie." Belle introduced the familiar strangers.

Billy had her arms around Sissy and Zoey and they held their breath, wondering how this was going to play out. Polly stood with them, still puzzled, but touched by the emotional scene.

Gracie waited this time for Eva to make the first move and the look on her face reminded Belle of a puppy waiting to be tossed a bone.

"Nice to meet you Miss Gracie," Eva's voice was steady as she shook Gracie's hand formally.

Gracie was hurt that Eva didn't give her a hug instead. "Well, baby, don't you remember me? I'm your..."

Eva spoke with purpose over the top of Gracie's words to stop her from finishing the sentence. "I know who you are but I'm thinking the only way, we're going to get through this is to pretend we're just meeting for the first time and see where things go from here."

Gracie released Eva's hand slowly, staring at the girl who proved to be a mature young lady. Her eyes moistened and her voice cracked like thin glass. "All right then, however you need to do this, Baby, uh, Eva. I hope someday we can become friends at least."

Eva remained unmoved and Gracie looked at Belle, "You've done a fine job, Belle, a fine job."

Without another word, she staggered home where the tears were allowed to flow freely and for the first time in her life, Gracie was severely stricken by her conscience.

* * *

TWENTY-NINE

"Belle, you need to get over here pronto. There is something we need to talk about and it has waited long enough!" Billy sounded urgent on the telephone.

"Is it all right if the girls come with me? They've been feeling kind of insecure since Sanford moved in with Gracie," Belle said.

"Well yes, but we'll have to find something for them to do so we can speak privately. Just hightail it over here, please!"

"OK, I've got Sanford's truck, so we won't be long. Is Zoey all right?" Belle wondered what was wrong, due to the panic in Billy's voice.

"Yes, yes, she's just fine. We'll see you soon." Billy hung up the phone.

"Well that was weird," Belle muttered, rushing down the porch steps. "Girls, let's go! We're headed for Miss Billy's!" she hollered to Eva and Sissy who were just finishing up their chores.

"OK, Mama!" Eva hollered back, tossing the metal bucket into the grain barrel.

Sissy closed and latched the barn door and the girls raced each other to the truck, arguing who was going to get to sit beside Belle on the way over.

When they arrived at Billy's, she met them at the front door. "Oh, Belle, I'm just so glad you could come. Forgive me for sounding so crazy on the phone but I just feel awful I've waited this long to tell you."

"Why don't you two play outside for a while?" Belle told Eva and Sissy when she saw how agitated Billy was.

"Stay where we can see you from the window," Billy added.

The girls did as they were told and Belle followed Billy inside. Zoey was in the kitchen, filling the tea pot with hot water. Belle noticed she was acting just as nervous as Billy was. "Hey Zoe," she greeted her.

"Oh, hey, Belle can I take your coat," she asked distractedly.

"No thanks I'll keep it on. What is it? You both seem so upset." Belle followed Billy into the living room and sat down on the sofa next to her as Zoey brought in the tray of refreshments.

Zoey hurried back into the kitchen and Billy poured Belle a cup of tea, setting it on a coaster on the coffee table. "Listen, Belle, there's something we've got to show you. Now don't get all bent out of shape that we didn't tell you sooner, because we thought it was best to wait." Billy fidgeted.

Belle blew on her tea. "What in the world is wrong with you two? You're acting like you got into a mess of chiggers!" She laughed. "Besides, who am I to get mad about not telling something when I should?"

"Belle, we got some letters." Billy started.

Zoey dried her hands on a dish towel and went to join them in the living room when an unexpected rap came at the door, making her shriek.

Billy turned to see what was wrong. "What the hell, Zoe? You want me to answer it?" She figured Manson wouldn't risk coming around in the middle of the day boldly announcing his arrival by knocking on the door.

Zoey was embarrassed to be startled so easily. "My nerves are just standing on end. I'll get it." She giggled at herself and opened the door to see Officer Owens standing in front of her.

"So we meet again. How can we help you this time?" Billy stood from the sofa to join Zoey.

"Well, ma'am, I'm just checking the area for you know who, again. Under the circumstances we're recommending folks keep their children home on Halloween instead of letting them go trick-or-treating," he nodded toward Eva and Sissy.

"Instead of making the kids miss out on their fun why don't you try looking inside the Buhler place, I mean, go in and actually *search* it," Billy retorted impatiently.

He grinned at her audacity. "Why, they teach my kids in Sunday school, ma'am. How could you think such a thing of such nice Christian ladies?"

She shook her head in disbelief that anyone could still believe the best of the Buhler's.

"Well, if you're so sure they're so nice, why don't you prove me wrong?" Billy continued to challenge him.

Belle listened as she watched Eva and Sissy chase each other around the fruit trees outside before joining her friends at the door, "What's going on, Bill?"

Billy was frustrated with the timing of his visit. "Like I said, we have a lot to talk about, Belle."

"I need to know if any of you have seen this man around." He held up the photograph of Manson for Belle to see it.

Belle yanked it from the officer's hand. "Manson? Why would you think we've seen him? He hasn't been around these parts for years!"

"Don't you know we've been asking about this man for months now? We tried to inform everyone out here in the sticks door to door. Guess we must have missed you." He shrugged.

"I guess so!" Belle realized Billy and Zoey weren't surprised at all to have the sheriff standing on their front porch.

"We've been keeping our eyes out for him for many years, of course, but he seemed to disappear for quite a spell. Now we're getting a lot of phone calls from folks saying he's been seen around town," he explained.

"Yeah, and one of those places folks have seen him is the Buhler house. I hear you even got a call from Doc Phelps. If you don't believe her, you won't believe, anybody!" Billy spat.

"Look, we went by there and talked to Miss Buhler and she said she hadn't seen him but if she did, she would be happy to let us know. We had no good reason to search her place. Well, I'll get out of your hair now. Give us a call if you see him, please." He turned to leave, just as Eva and Sissy ran up the steps to see what all the excitement was about. "I almost forgot. Ma'am, if I could just have that back I'd appreciate it." He reached for the photo in Belle's hand.

"Mama, why are you holding a picture of the nice man that helps me make my mud houses?" Sissy squealed, when she saw Manson's mug.

The blood drained from Belle's head, down to her toes and her color turned pallid.

"Excuse me, little lady. Are you saying you know this man?" Officer Owens held it closer so she could get a better look.

"Yes, sir he plays with me down by the lake where we live," Sissy replied.

"What, when? I always keep an eye on you and I've never seen him with you before!" Belle shook with fear.

"He stays in the trees and gets the twigs for me, Mama," Sissy explained, as if Belle should have figured that out already.

Belle shuddered, as the officer led her to the hallway where they could talk privately. "I need your address and telephone number. We're going to have to set up a team out at your place, ASAP."

Belle wrote down the information on his business card and handed it to him, then followed him back to the entryway.

"Can you tell me when your friend might be coming back to see you again?" He asked Sissy politely, not wanting to alarm her.

"I don't know. He just shows up sometimes," she replied nonchalantly.

"We'll be in touch." He tipped his hat to them and trotted down the steps.

"Girls, I want you to stay inside now. Why don't you go to the guestroom and read some books while we visit a spell," Belle instructed them, trying not to show how shaken she was. The girls were cold, so they didn't argue and went willingly to the bedroom shedding their coats and mittens along the way.

"Oh dear lord, where have I been, how could he be so close to my baby and I not even know it?" Belle agonized.

"You've been going through a lot lately, Belle. Besides, we all know how sneaky Manson can be," Billy soothed her.

"Why do I get the feeling you two already knew Manson was hanging around? Why didn't you tell me?" Belle felt tired all of a sudden.

"You haven't exactly kept in touch until lately, Belle," Billy said. "There's something else you don't know though and I'm just going to get right to it before we have any more interruptions." She went to her bedroom, returning with the letters from Ronny, holding the first one out to her.

Belle's mind raced and her pulse quickened, "Dear God, dear God, when did you get this?"

Zoey stood next to Billy, wringing her hands. "Well, we got that one a month or two ago."

"And you didn't tell me?" Belle asked incredulously.

Billy raised an eyebrow, thrusting the next letter on top of the first one. "I think we've covered that part of it, Belle. No, we didn't tell you. We got this one just a few weeks back. We tried to tell you when the girls were sleeping but they came into the room remember?"

Belle scanned each letter so quickly the words started to blur and she was unable to focus. "Read it to me, Billy. Please," she begged, as her eyes filled with water.

Billy read both letters aloud. "That's it, Belle. We wrote her back and told her you were with Sanford and she asked us not to tell you we heard from her. We were busting at the seams wanting to say something after you and Sanford split, but you can see why we didn't, can't you?"

Belle came to her senses. "I don't blame you two. Of course you did what you had to do, but she needs me. I have to go and see her right away. Was there a return address on the envelope?" Her head was spinning and thoughts raced through her mind much too quickly. She just couldn't think straight.

Billy handed the envelopes to her. "Yes, Belle, it's right here. She's not too awful far away."

Belle was numb. "You mean she's been living as close as Hannibal, and I never even knew it?" They stayed quiet, letting her process the bittersweet news. "I have to go to her." Belle couldn't seem to move fast enough.

"We know that, but what about the girls?" Billy helped her sort through the details.

"Sanford can stay with them at the house. But how can I possibly think of leaving when I know Manson's sniffing around?" Belle struggled with her conscience.

"Belle, Sanford won't let anything happen to the girls, you know he'd rather kill Manson as look at him. The police are going to be hiding out at your place anyhow and we'll be here to help in any way San needs us to. Hell, Eva and Sissy can even stay here with us if need be." Billy made it all sound so easy.

Belle held the silver locket that hung freely outside of her collar, between her fingers and closed her eyes. "I'm coming for you, Ron, hang on, I'm coming."

* * *

THIRTY

Belle rolled out the gingerbread, while Sissy stamped the dough with the cookie cutter before laying the men on their backs to be baked in the oven.

Joe stood at the stove, shaking the Jiffy Pop back and forth over a hot flame with Eva standing next to him, melting a stick of butter in a dented soup pan.

"Girls, Joe, I need to talk to you about something important." Belle turned off the stereo in the middle of Doris Day's "Secret Love." "Sissy, why don't you put that last pan of cookies on a platter and Joe, if you'd toss that corn and butter in this bowl and bring them into the living room, I'd sure appreciate it," Belle instructed them.

They hurried with their assigned tasks, wanting to hear what Belle had to say. Eva sat on the sofa with Joe on the arm next to her and Sissy sat next to her mother.

"What is it, Mama?" Eva asked, biting the head off a little brown man. She was in a much better mood since she and Joe had worked things out.

"I was wondering how you might feel about spending a little time with your daddy for a while." Belle began slowly.

"You too Mama," Sissy asked naively, thinking she meant they would all be together again.

"No, sweetheart, I mean just the three of you. You see, I need to take a trip. What I mean is you remember my best friend I told you about, the one that meant so much to me in school? Well, I found out where she's living and she needs my help getting back home. I know it's sudden, but I'm leaving first thing in the morning," she tried to explain carefully.

Sissy whined, "I don't want you to go away, Mama."

Eva looked a little bit like a mouse being backed into a corner. "I'm just not ready to spend that kind of time with Gracie, Mama. No offense, Joe."

He took Eva's hand, holding it tenderly in his. "I understand. No offense taken."

Belle realized how difficult it must be for her daughters, and the truth was she felt terrible just thinking about being away from them. Especially now, that Manson was on the prowl.

"No Eva, I wouldn't ask, you to neither. I already talked to your daddy about it and he's going to stay right here in the house with you while I'm gone." Belle could see they needed time to think it over but she didn't have much time left.

"Daddy's going to be living here again? I guess that would be OK." Sissy decided.

"Only while I'm gone and I won't be gone long." Belle reassured her. Eva was thinking it over. "How about you, sweetheart, you're being awful quiet. I know everything is so different than it's ever been for us but I really do need to go."

"I suppose if we're going to be staying here with Daddy that makes it all right with me. How long will you be gone?" Eva asked.

"No longer than a day or two. I plan on getting there and getting back and I promise I'll call you." Belle put their minds at ease.

Eva and Sissy nodded their heads in agreement. "OK, Mama," Eva answered for both of them.

"Don't you worry, Miss Belle, I'll be around often enough making sure these two stay out of trouble," Joe riled them. Eva giggled, and smacked him on the leg.

"All right you two, now that's settled, whose turn is it to start reading?" Belle held the book *Little Women* in the air.

"Mine, Mama," Sissy squealed. She loved this time of night when they all gathered together to read a good story.

"Wait. Mama, I have something I think may be very special. I've been waiting for the right time to give it to you and I feel like that time is now," Eva interrupted.

"Well, for heaven's sake, child, you sound so mysterious." Belle grinned.

It was obvious they needed some privacy, so Joe said, "Hey, Sissy. You know what we're missing? Hot cocoa, what say you and me go into the kitchen and make some?"

Sissy loved to do anything with Joe, so she followed him like a complacent puppy.

"Wait here, I'll be right back." Eva ran past Belle to her bedroom. She returned holding a small white box with a simple red ribbon tied around it. "Merry early Christmas, Mama."

Belle examined the tiny gift, eyeing Eva suspiciously as she opened it. She gasped when she saw the tarnished and weathered silver heart lying on a fluffy cotton pillow. The mere touch of the metal made the hair stand up on the back of her neck. "Where, pray tell, did you find this, Eva?"

"I found it under the tree house you and your friend Ronny were building by the church," Eva explained.

"How could you know anything about that? I haven't been there in ages myself." Belle couldn't take her eyes off the small ornament.

"Billy and Zoey told me about it then I found it when I went snooping around after Buhler kicked me out of VBS. I saw it on the ground and I grabbed it thinking it was yours." Eva hoped she had done the right thing by not showing her mother until now.

Belle muttered somberly, "It must have come off during the struggle between Ronny and her da... Manson. Thank you, Eva. There is no better gift you could have given me, other than bringing me Ronny herself. It's a sign, you know. It's a sign that we're going to be together again soon." Belle kissed her daughter on the cheek and put the locket around her neck to lay with her own. "Joe, Sissy? Come on now, it's, story time!" Belle hollered enthusiastically.

Sissy brought four ceramic mugs and Joe carried a carafe full of hot chocolate. "Well, it must have been good news because you're glowing, Miss Belle," Joe commented.

Sissy began reading but Belle was so distracted, she missed the part of the story where a boy named Laurie falls in love with a girl named Jo.

* * *

THIRTY-ONE

Belle kissed the girls while they slept and was just leaving them a note when Sanford knocked softly on the door early the next morning.

"Sit down for a cup?" Belle invited him in.

"Don't mind if I do." Sanford sat in his favorite spot at the table. "Here, I bought you a little something at Junior's on the way over." He reached inside his jacket and pulled out a ten-cent map with **Missouri** printed boldly across the front.

Belle grinned, "Thanks, big spender you know I'll need it." They chuckled together. "I appreciate you coming to stay with the girls while I'm gone. Hope it didn't cause any trouble between you and Gracie." Belle was sincere.

"Hey, Belle, it's our girls first, no matter what. Always will be," Sanford replied.

Eva and Sissy came down the hallway rubbing the sleep from their eyes and raced toward Sanford when they saw him sitting at the kitchen table drinking coffee with their mother, just like old times. "Daddy," they squealed in unison.

"Well, just how late were you two going to sleep today?" he teased, kissing each of them on the cheek and hugging them close, while trying not to spill his coffee.

"Is it true you're going to be staying here with us while Mama's gone, Daddy?" Sissy asked excitedly.

"Sure enough is, pumpkin," Sanford confirmed.

"Well, I best be getting on my way. I hate to leave but I'll be back soon enough," Belle promised.

"We're going to miss you, Mama." Eva hugged and kissed her mother good-bye.

"I love you, Mama," Sissy cried, not wanting to turn Belle loose. Her stomach ached when she realized she had never been any farther away from her mother than Miss Billy and Zoey's house before.

"I love you too, babies," Belle reassured them on her way out the door. Sanford followed her out and she threw her bags into the back of his pickup before settling herself behind the wheel. "What will you do for a car, San?" She pulled the belt snuggly across her lap and adjusted the seat to be closer to the steering wheel.

"Don't worry about me. Joe's coming by after work to give me one of the trucks from the mill. Now listen, Belle, the gun is loaded if you find you need it for any reason." Sanford referred to the hunting rifle he kept secured behind the seat. "I don't like the idea of you being out on the road alone without some kind of protection. Especially, now that we know Manson's hanging around. He could be anywhere. Keep your eyes open."

"All right, Sanford, but I'm sure I'll be just fine." She appreciated him looking out for her.

"I know you will, without a doubt. Now go on and bring your girl home. I'll hold down the fort here." Sanford closed the door and pushed the lock.

"Keep our girls safe. Manson's been hanging around Sissy down by the picnic table." She pointed down toward the lake when they noticed the bushes were moving.

"Something's down there. Wait here, Belle." Sanford whispered, taking the rifle from behind the seat. He moved swiftly down the bank toward the unseen culprit, aiming into the bushes. "Come on out of there, Manson. It's over."

A man wearing fatigues stood slowly with his hands in the air. "It's just us. We told your wife we'd be setting up down here. Didn't she tell you?"

Sanford lowered his gun and shook the officer's hand. "Sorry. Guess we expected a phone call first. Anyhow, we're glad you're here." He noticed three other men with guns wearing camouflage squatting in the brush. "Well, I'll leave you to it." He nodded and walked back up the hill.

"Who is it, Daddy?" Eva asked from behind the screen door.

"It's nothing, girls, but I want you two to stay away from the lake for a while. It's hunting season and I don't want you getting hurt," Sanford fibbed.

Belle understood they were the good guys sent to protect her loved ones and she was visibly relieved.

They said their final good-byes and she drove away, leaving the reflection of her family waving in the rearview mirror.

* * *

It had been a long day of driving before Belle was finally sitting in front of the Montgomery home, pulling the envelopes from her coat pocket to compare the address with the one made of brass on the front of the elegant home.

No one answered when she knocked on the door so she shuffled through the fallen leaves to sit in a swing while she waited, taking in the beautiful scenery. It wasn't long before a Lincoln Continental came into view and Belle thought she was dreaming when she saw a curly-headed woman leap out the back door, not waiting for the car to come to a complete stop.

"Blue! Is it truly you?" Ronny stumbled a bit then sprinted across the yard toward Belle, wrapping her arms around the love she had longed for.

Belle could hardly speak. "Yes, Ronny, it's me and I will never let you go, ever again."

Tears streamed down their cheeks. Ronny didn't hesitate to sit on Belle's lap and they clung tightly to one another as Harold and Hazel watched from the circle drive, a little misty eyed at the site of them.

"Let's go inside and give them some privacy, Harold," Hazel suggested over the lump in her throat.

"Good idea, Haze." Harold grabbed Belle's bags from the back of the truck and carried them into the house.

"How did you ever find me, Blue?" Ronny ran her fingers through Belle's hair.

"Billy and Zoey showed me the letters, Ron. They tried to keep them a secret like you asked them to but they knew I needed to know. Everyone back home can't wait to see you again." She wondered where to begin after so many years, when the words purged themselves without thought. "I'm just so sorry, Ron. I tried so hard to find you, but I just ran out of places to look. I hoped that if I stayed put, you would find your way home to me."

"I know, Blue. I carried a lot of guilt about not being able to get home to you too but there are good reasons nobody could find me. Manson hid us out in a place nobody even knew existed except him and the junkie that gave it to him. It's Manson's fault, Blue, not ours and we can't ever forget that." Ronny had learned to put the blame where it belonged.

Belle held her tight. "I should have knocked him upside the head with my hammer when he took you that day but it all happened so fast."

"There was nothing either one of us could have done. Now we've found one another and we have to focus on putting Manson away. Doc Callahan and Doc Snyder, she's my counselor say they know he abused me my whole life. They're both ready to tell the judge so too, if we ever go to court."

"Ron, there's something I need to tell you. I have two beautiful daughters back home and they can't wait to meet you." Ronny smiled, but Belle hesitated.

"What is it, Blue?" Ronny could tell she was hedging.

"Manson's been out at our place stalking my youngest." Belle spoke cautiously, not knowing how Ronny would take the news.

"What? Oh no, Blue! He's pure evil! Someone has to look out for your girls! Did he touch them? I swear to God..."

"Don't worry, Ron. The police have set a trap for him." Ronny heaved a sigh of relief as Belle continued. "Sanford's staying at the house too. He won't let, anything happen to them, you know that." Ronny stood from Belle's lap. "What's the matter?"

"Nothing, I'm just thinking," Ronny spoke softly and looked away.

"It's obvious something's bothering you. I know you, Ron. Talk to me," Belle said.

"What about Sanford, Blue? You're a married woman, no longer mine," Ronny assumed.

Belle took her hand, pulling her gently back onto her lap. "Sanford and I aren't together anymore, Ron. He knows I came to bring you home. Besides, he moved in with Gracie a long time ago."

Ronny's face brightened. "You mean it, Blue?"

"I mean it. We can talk about all of that later but for now, just know there's nothing left to keep us apart. And Ron, I have always belonged to you."

No more words were necessary when Ronny wrapped her arms around Belle's neck and they kissed each other like lovers do.

They entered the house flushed and rosy cheeked from the excitement of being together again. Harold and

Hazel were preparing supper and the smell of cinnamon and hot apple cider welcomed them in from the cold.

"Harold, Hazel, this is Blue Belle, my best friend in the whole wide world," Ronny introduced them.

"It's just lovely to meet you, Blue, we're so glad you could come. What a wonderful miracle you two have found one another again." Hazel smiled.

"Nice to meet you, Blue." Harold shook Belle's hand before ladling the cider into the mugs he had already set on the table. "You know you're welcome to stay as long as you like."

Blue and Ronny took a seat at the table. "I appreciate that, Mr. Montgomery, but I need to get home as soon as I can. You see, Manson's been snooping around our place and I need to get home to my girls," Belle explained, stirring her cider with a cinnamon stick.

"Oh my goodness, I know you're just worried sick about them!" Hazel exclaimed.

"Yes, ma'am," Belle replied simply.

Harold was quiet as he crushed the heart of a head of lettuce with the palm of his hand. Hazel knew what he was thinking but she didn't say anything as she took the lasagna out of the oven.

"You'll be going with her then, honey?" he asked without turning around to face them.

"Well, yes, right, Blue?" Ronny looked to her for confirmation.

"It's up to you, Ron, but at the same time, I'm not leaving here without you." Belle gently squeezed Ronny's hand.

Harold put the salad on the table and sat down while Hazel buttered the garlic bread.

"I'm not so sure any of this is such a good idea. If Manson's been spotted at your place, I think Ronny would be much safer here with us." He knew he was grasping at straws.

Hazel sat down next to him and laid her hand on top of his. "Ronny has Blue to help her now, Harold, and we need to get out of their way." Harold grimaced at the thought of Ronny leaving.

"I promise I'll be just fine. Besides, Blue Belle has always been good with a gun when she's needed to be. Isn't that right, Blue?" Ronny reassured him.

"You were never such a bad shot yourself, Ron." Belle smiled.

Harold hated to think of them needing to use a gun for any reason but he gave in reluctantly, realizing it was time for Ronny to move on and live her life. "You're part of this family, like a daughter to us, you know that." He looked fondly at her.

"Yes, sir and you're the only parents I've ever had." She hugged Harold and Hazel and Belle considered how blessed Ronny was to have found such paternal love at a time when she needed it most. They ate in silence, with much on their minds about the many changes ahead for all of them.

"Why don't you two let Blue and I clean up?" Ronny offered, when they had all finished eating.

"We just might take you up on that," Harold accepted through a great yawn.

"We'd like to get to bed a little early tonight, so yes that would be nice if you're sure, honey," Hazel added.

"We're sure." Belle said, standing to hug the Montgomery's. "I know words aren't enough to tell you how thankful I am that you've been taking such good care of my Ronny, but I'm so grateful you came along when you did."

"Well, you are most welcome and you know it has been our pleasure. Seems to us it was all just meant to be. You two ladies have a nice evening, now," Hazel said, as she and Harold headed up the stairs.

"I think we've decided to go for a walk," Ronny added.

"Oh that sounds splendid. Have fun, and make sure you bundle up, now." Hazel mothered them from the top of the stairs.

"Yes, ma'am," They sang in unison like two little school girls and giggled when they heard themselves.

Once the table was cleared and the dishes were washed, they wrapped scarves around their necks and zipped up their jackets before stepping out into the frosty air.

"It's as if we never parted, Ron." Belle said, as they each chose a swing, holding hands as they moved gently back and forth.

"I know. Being with you now is as natural as it's always been, Blue. I missed you so much I wanted to die and now it's like we haven't skipped a beat. Isn't that something?" Ronny observed happily.

"Yep, that is something." Belle felt complete for the first time since they parted.

They talked and laughed easily with one another, aiming to catch up on a lifetime spent apart. They cried together when Ronny shared the torture she had endured and Belle vowed silently to kill the malicious beast.

They stood, walking hand in hand in the light of the full moon. When they reached the edge of the forest, a tiny rabbit startled them when it hopped across their path and disappeared over the hill and they fell into a fit of laughter.

Belle snapped a twig from a bush, peeled several layers of bark from it then braided two soft strands together. "Will you give me your hand for a minute, Ron?" she asked softly.

"I'll give you my hand forever." Ronny held her right hand up for Belle to slide the organic ring onto her middle finger.

"Good because I'll take nothing less," she replied.

Ronny made an identical ring for Belle and placed it onto her finger of the same hand.

"Never again will we part and always will we be the truest of companions," Belle recited from the pages of her heart.

God herself was the only witness to this simple ceremony and Ronny's eyes filled with tears as they shared a tender kiss, delighting in the spirit of love.

* * *

THIRTY-TWO

"Mama," Eva and Sissy rushed down the porch steps to give their mother a hug when they heard the truck pull into the drive. Joe waited on the steps, giving them a few moments to say hello.

"My girls, I wasn't gone too long now, was I?" Belle asked, holding them close. "Ronny, would you ever have guessed these were my babies?" Belle stood back to eye them proudly.

"Well, of course, I would. It's so nice to finally meet you both," Ronny greeted them.

"Nice to meet you," They each took a turn greeting her warmly.

"And I *know* you'll never guess who this one is." Belle pointed at Joe.

"You had a boy too, Blue?" Ronny teased.

Joe joined them in the driveway to shake Ronny's hand. "Hi, Miss Ronny. I'm Joe, Gracie's son."

"Joe, you were supposed to make her work a little harder at guessing." Belle laughed.

Ronny wrinkled her nose, not quite knowing what to say. "You mean *Gracie,* Gracie? But..."

"Yeah, I know, I'm a white boy." Joe beat her to the punch and everyone laughed at the surprised expression on Ronny's face. "Well, I don't know about you folks, but I'm freezing! He rubbed his hands together briskly and grabbed their bags from the bed of the truck before following them inside.

Belle had called the girls the night before to tell them she and Ronny would be home the next day, so Eva and Sissy had chili and fresh-from-the-oven corn bread ready for a late dinner.

Joe poked the log in the fireplace. "Well, I best be getting to the mill," he said with a kiss to Eva's cheek, wishing he could stay.

"Uh, Joe, could you bring those bags up to my room, please?" Belle asked him, needing an excuse to talk privately.

"Happy to," he said, hauling them down the hallway.

Belle met him at the bottom of the stairs that led to her room. "Any sign of Manson?"

"Afraid not, Miss Belle, Sanford stayed here all night and I came, this morning. The police are still down by the lake," he explained.

"Knowing you and Sanford were here gave me such peace of mind that I could go get Ronny. Thank you, Joe." Belle hugged him.

"That's all right, glad to do it." He looked down the hallway with raised eyebrows. "Besides, now that I see how pretty she is, I know why you had to run out of here so fast yesterday," he kidded her.

"Joe. You are something terrible." she joked back, whacking him on the shoulder.

He winced, "Dang! Why are you Johnson women always beating on me?" They both laughed out loud, and Joe took the bags upstairs.

Ronny and the girls were visiting and getting acquainted when Belle came back into the kitchen. "Sounds like you two were having a good time back there." Ronny grinned.

"Well, once you get to know Joe, you'll see he has a better sense of humor than his mother does." She chuckled, taking a seat next to Ronny. Joe came back into the kitchen. "Can you stay for lunch?" Belle invited him.

"Wish I could but Mr. Farnsworth gave me the morning as it is to stay here with the girls until you got home. Now I've got to get back to it," he explained. "I'll run Sanford out after work. He wants to say hi to Miss Ronny. He'll get the truck then. Nice meeting you, ma'am," Joe nodded his head to Ronny.

Everyone said good-bye as he took Eva's hand and she walked outside with him where they shared a real kiss and he went to work, leaving her walking on cloud nine.

"Nice young man," Ronny commented when Eva returned.

"Yes, ma'am, isn't he though?" Eva swooned.

"Joe and Eva sitting in a tree..." Sissy sang with a mouthful of chili.

"You better watch it," Eva growled at her sister.

"All right, you two, what must Ronny think of you fighting like that?" Belle hoped to break up the quarrel before it got too far out of hand like she knew it could.

"Yes, ma'am," they replied out of habit.

"You two are lucky to have one another to argue with. I never had a sister. Why, I'm almost jealous." Ronny winked at them, buttering her second piece of corn bread.

"Would you like some honey on that, Ron?" Belle asked, sliding the bear closer to her.

"Good lord, yes. But I'm going to get so fat if I keep eating like this, I swear!" She said as, she drizzled some honey into her chili as well as onto her bread. Eva and Sissy were shocked to see someone do such a thing and they looked saucer eyed at one another, knowing they liked her right away.

"Same old Ron, thank goodness. You're as bad as Sissy," Belle teased, watching Ronny eat a spoonful of honey-drenched chili.

They laughed and talked and when they were finished eating, they cleared the table and washed up. Eva went to put more wood on the dwindling fire while Sissy sat on the sofa to read a good book.

Belle and Ronny washed and stacked the dishes in the plastic drainer that sat on the counter at the edge of the sink. "You smell smoke, Ron?" Belle sniffed the air.

"Well yeah, it's coming from the fireplace isn't it?" Ronny replied, drying a plate with the dish towel.

"Huh. I guess you're right. Let's leave those to dry and go sit by the fire." Belle stood belly to belly with Ronny and wrapped her arms around her waist.

"Sounds good to me," Ronny smiled, and they kissed.

"Eva, put some good music on the turntable will you?" Belle asked when they entered the living room. "Wait just a minute. What's that sound? Is that Bessie hollering outside?" Belle stopped to listen. "Something isn't right. I'm going to go see what's going on. You stay here with the girls, Ron."

Belle put on her jacket and walked outside to see smoke coming from the barn and the cows running in circles, bellowing and bumping into one another, trying to get away from the scorching flames. The chickens hopped up and down wishing they could fly and scattered as they screeched for help.

Belle ran toward the corral and opened the gates, setting the livestock free. She coughed as the smoke filled her lungs and her blood curdled when she felt his eyes on her. "Manson!"

"You ain't supposed to be here, bitch! I was plannin' on spendin' some alone time with your daughters but they ain't been out and about lately for some reason. I s'pose those pigs down there in the trees got somethin' to do with it, huh?" He mocked her through the smoke and rising flames.

Belle thought she was going to be sick just thinking of him being anywhere near, her daughters. "You will never get close to my babies again! I'll kill you first! Why don't you just turn yourself in and save yourself some jail time?"

"Now, do I look stupid to you? We both know if I go back to jail, ain't no way they're gonna ever let me out. That's why I ain't never, goin' back," he vowed vehemently. "By the way, you look pretty good in your birthday suit." He sneered.

Belle remembered the day she thought someone was watching her swim and she pulled her jacket tighter around her; disgusted to think he had seen her that way. She hoped the policemen were hurrying up the hill as she ignored his comment, trying to stall for time.

"Just what is it you want, anyhow?" Belle tried to sound like she cared.

"Revenge," His tone smacked of bitterness and he disappeared into the shadows of the thick smoke.

Ronny called the fire station and rushed out the door with Eva and Sissy right behind her. "Belle, what's happened? Are you all right?"

The police surrounded the burning barn hunting Manson with their guns aimed ready to kill him as the sound of sirens peeled through the air.

"It's Manson, Ronny! He was here, he set this fire!" Belle hollered, gasping for air.

Ronny led her away from the commotion as the red trucks parked and hosed the flames down, snuffing the fire out within minutes.

"Eva girl, let's get you into the house where it's warm." Belle noticed she didn't have a coat on. "Where's Sissy?"

"She was right behind me when we came out of the house, Mama," Eva replied.

Panic set in as Belle and Ronny each had the same terrible thought as the other and they saw the trail of dust in the air that could only come from a car speeding through gravel. "He must have hidden the car in the trees!" Belle yelled as they ran toward the house.

"Sissy, Sissy!" They yelled, searching frantically for her inside.

"Oh dear God, he's taken her!" Belle's stomach was tied in knots as three police officers entered the house.

"Where the hell, were you, you were supposed to protect my family! What took you so long? He was right here, and now he has my baby!" she screamed at them as Ronny held her hand for support.

"Belle, we got up here as soon as we could. Now listen, are you saying you saw Manson and he has taken your daughter?" Officer Owens asked in a mild tone, hoping to calm her.

"Yes, Sissy, she's gone. She was here and then gone when Manson disappeared!" Belle held her stomach, wanting to puke.

"Is this the same little girl I met at Miss Billy's place the other day, ma'am?" he asked.

Belle looked at him as if just realizing who he was. "Yes, that's right," she replied weakly.

"Well, chances are she went with him willingly because she thinks of him as her playmate, her friend," he reasoned, but could see Belle didn't understand the significance of what he was saying. "The point is we can assume he hasn't done anything to harm her. He didn't have to use force to get her to go with him." He really did want to offer Belle some hope.

"We will find her, ma'am. Do you have a photograph we can use?" A female officer approached her gently.

Belle found a recent school picture on the desk, just as Sanford and Joe rushed through the door.

"Belle, We heard the sirens and came right away! What's happened?" He didn't know it was worse than losing the barn. Belle sobbed as she told him the news. Sanford went to Joe who was comforting Eva and whispered something in his ear. Joe nodded, and Sanford left without a word. Ronny watched him through the kitchen window as he pulled the rifle from behind the seat of his pickup, fishtailing through the gravel as he sped away.

* * *

THIRTY-THREE

"Who do you think you are taking Eunice's car like that and why in tar nation did you bring that girl here?" Beatrice spat.

"You don't worry, nothin' about it," Manson spoke passively, as he pushed Sissy through the living room and down the stairs to his makeshift apartment in the basement.

The little girl held her breath as he forced her arm up between her shoulder blades with one hand and grasped a handful of hair with the other, just like he had always done to Ronny.

Eunice watched from the shadows of the kitchen, crushed he had chosen yet another girl that wasn't her. *After all*

I've done to make him love me. I'll make him pay. She picked up the telephone and dialed.

Downstairs, Manson tied the young girl to the single bed with ropes he had already looped around each metal leg. "It's been a long time." He drooled as she stared up at him terror stricken.

He wanted to kiss the child but knew she would scream if he removed the duct tape from her mouth.

Swiftly, skillfully, the team of troopers swooped in, untied the young girl and carried her from the room before Manson could have even one more disgusting thought about what he wanted to do to her. The frigid metal at the base of his skull stopped him cold and he pissed his pants when Sanford pulled the trigger.

* * *

THIRTY-FOUR

Rosemary Clooney sang "Count Your Blessings" in the background, setting just the right mood for Earl's Thanksgiving toast. "I just want to say how much I appreciate friends such as you all." He raised his glass. "If it weren't for good people like you, I would have been alone on this holiday and I don't even want to know what that might have felt like without my Bonnie. So, here's to friendships and never having to feel the pain of loneliness."

"Hear, hear!" everyone declared in unison clinking, their glasses together before taking a sip of Champagne.

Zoey had slowly baked and butter basted the wild turkey Billy shot in the woods earlier that morning and the picked clean carcass sat on the platter as evidence that everyone had enjoyed it immensely. Besides the good tasting bird they had a blessed feast of cranberry salad, mashed potatoes, country gravy smooth as cream, boiled Chinese cabbage, fried okra, turnip greens, baking powder biscuits and melt in your mouth dumplings that went down easily with the help of brandy infused eggnog, sprinkled with cinnamon and nutmeg.

Polly raised her glass. "I would like to make a toast as well. How can I properly thank you folks for showing up without even being asked and jumping in to help me hold it all together when I wasn't able to do so by myself? You all are the very best friends anyone could ever have and I love every one of you like family."

"We feel the same way, Pol. Come here and give me a kiss!" Zoey was a little tipsy and grabbed Polly to hug her close and kissed her on the cheek.

"Since we're family, does that mean Zoey gets a discount now that you're back in business, Pol?" Billy heckled her ruthlessly.

"Billy? I can't believe you, woman of mine!" Zoey slung her cloth napkin through the air, pretending to whip Billy with it while everyone laughed heartily, feeling blessed to be in the company of such loving companions.

Eva grabbed a kiss from Joe before going outside to play hide and seek with Sissy and Polly's two daughters in the crisp fall air. The adults shared the task of cleaning the kitchen before gathering in the living room for their choice of pecan, sweet potato, and mince meat pie. Most decided on a small piece of all three.

Gracie sat next to Belle. "How are the girls doing, Belle?" she asked genuinely.

"Thanks to Sanford, they're doing just fine. It's good to see them out playing again without being afraid. Sissy still won't sleep alone and she sticks pretty close to Eva most of the time but she's a strong girl, she'll get there." Belle appreciated her interest in their welfare and Sanford smiled at Belle, glad she and Gracie were able to visit without any hard feelings between them.

"I can't believe Manson set my car on fire. I mean, why pick on me and Polly?" Earl interjected, licking the whipped cream out of his new mustache.

"The police found a list of our names in the Buhler's house. Apparently, Billy and Zoey were next. He was trying to get back at Ronny for setting him on fire, so he knew the best way to hurt her was to hurt the people she loves," Belle explained, sipping her coffee.

Ronny was standing with Harold and Hazel, looking out the window, noticing the persimmons that were covered in frost. "We are so glad you could join us for this Thanksgiving shindig," Billy said, handing the Montgomery's each a generous slice of pie.

"Who could turn down an invitation to Heaven? This place is beautiful," Harold exclaimed. "Are you sure you want to head out for Branson tomorrow, Hazel? Maybe we could stay here a few more days."

"Sounds good to me, Harold, maybe we can stay long enough for Billy and Zoey to teach me how they grow such a beautiful garden," Hazel complimented them.

"With a lot of love and hard work, Hazel, I don't know if Ron told you or not, but we host the WPFA meetings every month. You know, the Woman's Progressive

Farmers Association. We teach women how to grow a healthy garden and then how to preserve the harvest so they can feed their families even when times are tough."

"Well, I'll be. I didn't know the association still existed. My mother told me about it when I was just a young girl," Hazel mused.

"Yep, it's been going since 1928," Billy said proudly. "Matter of fact, we're having a meeting tomorrow afternoon. We'll be doing a seed exchange. If you'd care to join us, we'd love to have you," Billy invited her. "Excuse me a moment, Hazel, I see some folks are still needing dessert." She met Zoey in the kitchen to fill cups with coffee and saucers with pie.

"I know this is ornery, but I just love thinking of the Buhler biddies sitting in jail," Zoey admitted to Billy.

"I know Zoe, and isn't it funny how the two most religious folks in town managed to create the devil between them? Who would have thought, Reverend Dan and old Buhler, was ever doing the chicken dance together," They both cackled on their way to join the others.

The girls had come in from outside and Joe joined them in the back bedroom to play a game of Scrabble, while the old friends relaxed in the living room, getting acquainted and reacquainted, remembering old times and looking forward to new ones.

Belle whispered in Ronny's ear, "I have a surprise for you. Do you think we can slip out of here without causing too much of a commotion?"

"Sure. What about the girls?" Ronny replied.

"They're going to stay here with Billy and Zoey for a while." Belle took Ronny's hand and led her discreetly out of the room, grabbing their coats on their way out the front door.

No one noticed them leave except Sanford. He was grinning from ear to ear as he watched them from the window driving away in his pickup truck and decided then and there, he would give it to Belle for Christmas since she drove it more than he did anyway.

"Where are we going, Blue?" Ronny asked, as they drove through the deserted streets of town. "Everything's closed today, remember? It's Thanksgiving." She tried to get Belle to give her a hint.

"Just wait and see, just wait and see." Belle kept the secret until they pulled into the church parking lot.

Ronny's mind flashed back to the day Manson grabbed her and shoved her into his car. "What are we doing, Blue? I don't really like being here."

"It's OK, Ron. We're going to make some new memories today. Manson has no more power over us and we're going to finish what we started a long time ago." Belle took her hand and Ronny slid across the seat, following her out the driver's side.

They walked down a freshly groomed trail through the overgrown brush as the waiting tree, with the half-built house, beckoned them to come closer.

"Blue. Can you believe it's still here?" Ronny gasped.

"It's just been waiting for us, Ron. This is where I was the other day when you were showing Harold and Hazel around town. I cleared this path and, well, you'll see."

Ronny grabbed a wooden step and her pulse quickened with excitement as she climbed to the top, with Belle right behind her.

They took their boots off and Belle turned the old transistor radio to their favorite station before pulling Ronny gently onto the thick blankets and pillows she had made into a cozy bed.

They kissed passionately, unable to take their eyes off one another as Belle took something from her coat pocket.

"This is for you." She held the tiny white box with the red string out to her.

"What's this, Blue Belle?"

"Let's just say it's been waiting for you to come home to get it. Like me," Belle hinted mysteriously.

Ronny eyed her curiously before lifting the lid to see the locket she thought was lost forever. Awestruck, she traced the newly polished silver with her fingertip before popping the clasp to reveal two young girls, torn apart so long ago, only to be brought together again by the unseen forces of love and Providence. Without a word, Ronny held the chain up for Belle to hook it at her throat.

Julie London sang, "I Want You for Christmas" as the first snow began to fall and the reunited lovers tumbled under the blankets. Blue caressing Ronny, and Ronny embracing Blue.

* * *

Made in the USA
Lexington, KY
04 March 2010